KB067473

연애의 감정학

〈K-픽션〉 시리즈는 한국문학의 젊은 상상력입니다. 최근 발표된 가장 우수하고 흥미로운 작품을 엄선하여 출간하는 〈K-픽션〉은 한국문학의 생생한 현장을 국내외 독자들과 실시간으로 공유하고자 기획되었습니다. 〈바이링궐 에디션 한국 대표 소설〉 시리즈를 통해 검증된 탁월한 번역진이 참여하여 원작의 재미와 품격을 최대한 살린 〈K-픽션〉 시리즈는 매 계절마다 새로운 작품을 선보입니다.

The K-Fiction Series represents the brightest of young imaginative voices in contemporary Korean fiction. This series consists of a wide range of outstanding contemporary Korean short stories that the editorial board of *ASIA* carefully selects each season. These stories are then translated by professional Korean literature translators, all of whom take special care to faithfully convey the pieceså original tones and grace. We hope that, each and every season, these exceptional young Korean voices will delight and challenge all of you, our treasured readers both here and abroad.

연애의 감정학
How to Break Up Like a Winner

백영옥|제이미 챙, 신혜빈 옮김
Written by Baek Young-ok
Translated by Jamie Chang, Shin Hye-bin

ASIA
PUBLISHERS

차례
Contents

연애의 감정학
How to Break Up Like a Winner

1.

태희가 종수와 헤어진 건 1년 2개월 전이었다.

태희에겐 세 번째 이별이었다.

이별이 힘든 이유는 매번 늘어났다. 첫 번째 이별은 재수를 고려할 때라 그랬고, 두 번째 이별은 입사 후 첫 프로젝트 때문에 혼란스러웠다. 세 번째 이별에는 복병이 찾아왔다. 활짝 핀 목련과 흩날리는 벚꽃을 바라보며 세상 밖 풍경과 마음 속 계절이 이렇게 달라도 되나 싶었다. 퇴근길 지하철 플랫폼에서, 회사명이 적힌 설악산 워크숍 깃발 아래에서 "딱 한 발만 내디디면 이대로 갈 수도 있겠구나"란 생각이 멈추지 않았다. 야근이

1.

One year and two months had gone by since Tae-hee and Jong-su broke up.

This was Tae-hee's third breakup.

Breakups were hard for a number of reasons, and that number increased with each breakup. The first was hard because she was considering reapplying to college at the time, the second was a mess because she was in the midst of her first big project at work. The third blindsided her. Looking up at the magnolias in full bloom and cherry blossoms fluttering in the gentle winds, she marveled at the disparity between her external reality and her

반복되던 직장 4년 차 증상과 비슷했다.

로또에 당첨되면 가장 먼저 하고 싶은 일이 회사를 그만두는 건 아니었다. 언제든 그만둘 수 있다면 그곳이 더 이상 지옥은 아닐 테니까. 죽을 희망이 있다고 생각하면 어쩐지 마음이 놓였다. 사표를 노트북의 바탕화면 맨 위에 깔아놓고 늘 마음을 다잡았다.

"적응하면 괜찮아져."

친구 재연은 습관처럼 말했다. 하지만 적응하면 좋아지는 게 아니다. 적응하면 무뎌진다. 무뎌지면 아프지 않고, 아프지 않으면 괜찮아진 거라 착각한다. 밤새 먹어서 퉁퉁 부은 얼굴을 바라보던 날 아침, 태희는 괜찮지 않더라도 괜찮은 척 착각이라도 해야겠다고 생각했다. 그것이 자기 기만이든 자기 합리화든 상관없었다.

그날 이후, 한 시간 일찍 일어났다. 출근 전에 수영을 했다. 미뤄두었던 일본어 공부를 시작했고, 홍보물만 받아두었던 사내의 재테크 스터디 모임에 가입했다. 금요일 이른 퇴근 후에 발레 공연을 보기 위해 블라디보스톡행 비행기에 올라탔다. 마린스키 극장의 가장 좋은 좌석에 앉아서 매일 두 편 이상의 발레 공연을 봤다.

종수는 잘사는 것 같았다.

internal climate. Standing on the platform at the subway station at the end of the day, standing under the banner bearing the company name at the Seoraksan Mountain Retreat, she couldn't stop thinking: *One step forward, and it'll all be over*. She'd had similar symptoms on her fourth year at the company when she was working all hours of the day and night without time for a breather.

Quitting her job wasn't the first thing on her if-I-win-the-lottery wish list. Hell isn't hell if you can quit any time—knowing that death was an option restored peace in her heart. She moved "letter of resignation.docx" to the desktop of her laptop to self-soothe.

"You'll be fine once you get used to it," her friend Jae-yon liked to say. You don't get *used* to it; you get *numb* to it, more like. You get numb, the pain goes away, and you can delude yourself into thinking you're fine. One morning, as Tae-hee looked at her face bloated from a night of binge eating, she told herself she'd settle for deluding herself into thinking she was fine—self-aggrandizement, rationalization, whatever it took.

From that day on, she got up an hour early. She swam before work. She finally started taking Japa-

일주일 간격으로 그의 SNS 프로필 사진이 바뀌었다. 종수의 머리 색깔이 바뀌고, 한 번도 보지 못한 셔츠가 등장할 때마다, 태희는 수영장 트랙을 한 바퀴씩 더 돌았다. 숨이 차오를 때마다, 심장의 근육이 더 강해지고 있다고 믿었다. 보이지 않는 종수와 경쟁하는 기분이었지만 나쁘지만은 않았다. 헤어지고 두 달 후, 일본어 1급 자격증 시험을 통과했을 때, 퇴근길에 들었던 매미 울음소리에 여름이 깊어졌다는 걸 깨달았다.

"헤어지자마자, 다른 여자 사귀는 게 무슨 뜻이겠어?"

재연이 무심결에 내뱉은 이 얘길 듣기 전까지, 태희는 자신이 세 번째 이별을 잘 헤쳐나가고 있다고 생각했다. 정신적으로 이전보다 더 강해졌다고 느꼈다.

"이별하는 게 힘들었나 보지. 나도 그랬으니까."

태희는 최대한 담담하게 말하려 애썼다.

"양다리야."

"뭐?"

"이종수, 너랑 헤어지기 전부터 여자가 있었던 거라고."

이별의 이유가 바뀌는 순간이었다.

권태에서 외도로.

nese classes, and dug up the brochure for the Financial Investment Study Group at the company to attend a meeting. She took a half day on a Friday and flew off to Vladivostok to go to the ballet. She saw at least two performances each day over the weekend from the best seat in the Mariinsky Theatre.

Jong-su seemed to be doing just fine.

His profile pictures on his various social media changed weekly. Each time his hair color changed and a shirt she'd never seen him wear appeared in the pictures, Tae-hee added another lap to her morning swim. She took being out of breath as a sign that her heart muscles were getting tougher. She felt she was competing with an imaginary Jong-su, but it wasn't completely a bad feeling. Two months after the breakup when she passed the JLPT N1, she noticed that summer was marching on through the city as she headed home in the racket of wailing cicadas.

"What do you think it means when a guy starts up with a girl immediately after a breakup?"

Until Jae-yon threw this at Tae-hee without a thought in her head, Tae-hee had been satisfied with how well she was handling her third breakup. She was mentally stronger this time, or so she

여름이 깊어지고 있었다.

2.

태희는 모범생이었다.

뭐든 시도하고 배우는 걸 좋아했다. 학원으로 가는 버스와 자동차 안에서 끼니를 해결하며 영어 단어를 암기할 정도로 시간을 아낀 덕에, 그녀는 늘 상위권 성적을 유지했다. 태희는 강남의 사교육 프레임에 단련된 학생답게 모르는 게 있으면 늘 답을 찾아 나섰다. 그것이 무엇이든 일목요연하게 정리해 핵심을 짚는 일타강사가 있을 거란 믿음이 있었다. 입시 전이나 입사 후에도 마찬가지였다.

그렇게 진화심리학에 입각해 부장과 팀장의 기 싸움을 영장류들의 서열 다툼으로 해석했다. 행동경제학자들이 분석하듯 다툼을 '조정 문제'로 해석했다. 조선 시대 사극을 보는 기분으로 격렬한 사내 정치 중인 김 이사와 성 본부장 중, 누가 장희빈이고 인현황후인지를 가늠했다.

종수와의 연애 역시 그랬다.

손실기피, 자아고갈, 매물비용, 소유효과, 확증편향

thought.

"That the breakup was hard on him? It was hard for me, too," Tae-hee said with all the nonchalance she could summon up.

"Foul play."

"What?"

"Jong-su Lee was already seeing her before he broke up with you."

Right there: the moment the reason for their breakup changed.

From tedium to infidelity.

Summer, indeed, was marching on.

2.

Tae-hee was the quintessential student. She enjoyed trying and learning new things. Extremely economical with her time, she memorized English vocabulary over meals, which she took on the bus and in the car on the way to and from school and various tutors who kept her grades above the 90th percentile. Conditioned by the Gang-nam private education mill, her solution to all things beyond her grasp was to go looking for an explanation. Whatever the conundrum, she had faith there would be

같은 용어가 태희의 머리를 뒤덮었다. 그와 헤어졌을 때, 그녀는 억울해하거나 우는 대신 서점으로 달려갔다. 관련 서적을 샅샅이 살펴보고, 유튜브와 TED에 들어가 동영상들을 찾았다. 책과 강연의 제목을 살펴보는 것만으로 미처 볼 수 없었던 심리의 사각지대가 보일 것 같았다. 애착 유형으로 보는 연애 스타일, 내적 동기는 어떻게 찾아지는가, 나는 왜 나쁜 남자에게 끌리는가, 조용히 승리하는 방법, 결코 지지 않는 법······.

이기길 원했던 게 아니다.

지고 싶지 않았을 뿐이다. 승리의 기쁨은 강렬하지만 짧다. 졌을 때, 밀려났을 때, 떨어졌을 때 느껴지는 열패감은 길고 길어 각인된 흉터를 남긴다. 이별이 지는 것이라고 생각하면 견딜 수 없었다. 그래서 종수와 헤어지고 태희가 처음 했던 의식적인 행동은 자신의 SNS 계정에서 종수를 지우는 것이었다. 눈에 보이지 않으면 빨리 잊을 수 있다.

"종수, 누구 사귀는 줄 알아?"

재연의 입을 막는 대신, 자신의 귀를 틀어막고 싶었

a tutor somewhere who could give her a clear, step-by-step analysis and an irrefutable answer. This problem-solving approach persisted from school days through professional career.

At work, middle-management power play was analyzed through the framework of evolutionary psychology: they were primates attempting to establish a pecking order. Office disputes were interpreted, as behavioral economists would, as a "structuring issue." Like the audience of a period court drama, Tae-hee played spectator to the office bloodbath and tried to figure out which Trustee Kim or Branch Manager Seong was—Anne Boleyn or Catherine of Aragon?

Tae-hee applied the same approach to her relationship with Jong-su.

Terms like loss aversion, ego depletion, sunk cost, endowment effect, and confirmation bias flooded her head. When they broke up, instead of wallowing or crying, she headed straight for the bookstore. She scanned the self-help aisle and looked for lectures and TED talks on YouTube. Looking at the book and lecture titles was enough to make her feel she was getting to the bottom of her psychological blind spot: *Relationship Attachment*

다. 하지만 그럴 수 없었다.

"헤어지자마자 다른 사람과 연애하면 무조건 양다리야?"

태희가 재연을 보며 말했다.

뱃속 깊은 곳에서부터 점심에 급하게 먹은 뚝배기 미역국이 거대한 해파리처럼 내장기관을 차례로 휘감으며 돌아다니는 기분이었다. 펄펄 끓던 뚝배기 속 미역이 닿는 곳마다 화상을 당하는 것 같았다. 과거, 사소하게 지나쳤던 일들이 퍼즐처럼 맞춰지자 막연했던 고통의 내용이 날카롭게 선명해졌다.

"왜 그런 애들 있잖아? 상대가 먼저 지쳐 나가떨어지길 기다리는 사람들. 그래서 이종수가 헤어지기 몇 달 전부터 네 전화도 안 받고, 약속에 늦고, 매일 야근한다는 핑계를 댄 거야. 네 입에서 헤어지자는 말 나올 때까지 기다린 거야. 헤어지자고 말하면 자기가 나쁜 사람 되잖아. 헤어지는 그 순간까지도 자긴 멋진 사람이고 싶었던 거야. 결국 태희 네가 헤어지자고 한 거잖아. 헤어지자는 말도 자기가 못하는 사람이랑 뭘 하겠니? 그게 결정 장애가 아니면 뭐야?"

결정 장애가 아니었다.

Style, Get In Touch With Your Inner Motivation, Why Am I Attracted To Jerks?, The Path To Quiet Victory, The Secret To Never Losing.

Winning wasn't what she was after.

Only, she didn't want to lose. The thrill of victory is as intense as it is brief. The dejection of being bested, ousted, or declined goes on and on, impressing an indelible scar on one's being. She couldn't bear the thought of breaking up as a form of failure. So the first conscious action she took after the breakup was deleting Jong-su from her social media. Out of sight, briskly out of mind.

"Guess who Jong-su is going out with."

Tae-hee wanted to stuff her own ears instead of cupping a hand over Jae-Yon's mouth. But she couldn't do either.

"Going out with someone immediately after breaking up doesn't necessarily mean there was overlap," said Tae-hee, looking Jae-yon squarely in the eye.

From the bottom of her stomach, the seaweed in the bubbling hot stone pot soup Tae-hee scarfed down for lunch coiled around every one of her internal organs as it made its way back up, stinging

종수에게 선택의 개념이 달랐을 뿐이다. A와 B 중 하나를 배제하는 것이 아니라 둘 다를 갖는 게 선택이라고 생각하는 사람이 할 수 있는 가장 합리적인 선택을 한 것뿐이다.

"태희 넌 화도 안 나니? 걔 양다리라니까!"

종수의 양다리는 처음이 아니었다.

광고주 미팅에서 처음 만났던 종수에겐 여자 친구가 있었다. 에스프레소를 연달아 넉 잔을 마시는 카페인 중독자 이종수 대리에겐 3년이나 사귄 여자 친구가 있었다. 하지만 본격적으로 연애가 시작된 후에야 태희는 그 사실을 알아챘다.

그 일로 2주 동안 연락을 끊었었다.

종수에게 메시지가 온 건 일주일 후였다. 그녀와 헤어졌다는 장문의 문자였다. 거짓말을 했던 사람을 끝까지 믿어줄 아량이 자신에게 없다고 생각했다. 하지만 시간이 지날수록 종수가 한 거짓말보다 그 여자와 헤어져준 용기가 더 고마웠다. 그의 거짓말은 곧 용기로 포장됐다. SNS 계정에서 이종수를 삭제하던 순간, 그가 아직 자신을 친구로 놔둔 채 지우지 않았다는 것에 안도한 것만큼이나 자기 기만적이었다.

with its tentacles like an enormous jellyfish. The little things she ignored while they were together fell into place like puzzle pieces, bringing her pixelated pain into razor-sharp focus.

"You know the type," Jae-yon pressed on. "Guys who drag things out and make you break up with them. That's why he didn't answer your calls or show up on time for months leading up to the breakup—always with the same excuse: *I'm working late*. He was waiting for you to say the word. He didn't want to be the jerk who dumped the girl. He wanted to be the good guy to the very end. So *you* had to bring it up, Tae-hee. What do you do with a guy who can't even say the words, *Let's break up*? If that isn't indecisiveness, I don't know what is."

It was not indecisiveness. Jong-su had a different idea of what his choices were. To him, the options weren't A or B, but A, B, or both A and B. He went for the option that made the most sense to him.

"Why aren't you pissed, Tae-hee? He was cheating on you!"

Wouldn't be the first. Jong-su had a girlfriend when he met Tae-hee for the first time at an ad client meeting. Jong-su, a caffeine addict who knocked back four shots of espresso in one seating, had a

"믿지 못할 사람을 사랑하는 게 최악이야! 나쁜 자식!"

재연의 목에 핏대가 서는 게 보였다. 대신 화를 내주는 게 어쩌면 친구의 가장 큰 존재 의미인지도 모른다. 가끔 태희는 재연이 자신이 가진 또 다른 인격의 일부처럼 느껴졌다.

"누가 그러더라. 사랑은 믿는 거라고. 말 같은 소릴 하라고 해! 사랑하는 거랑 믿는 건 전혀 다른 문제라고. 사랑하는데도 상대를 믿지 못하는 사람이 얼마나 많은 줄 알아? 위치 추적 하고, 화상 통화로 수시로 어딨는지 확인하고. 애인 몰래 SNS랑 스마트폰, 이메일 체크하는 사람은 또 얼마나 많냐고. 이종수는 전형적인 회피성 애착이야. 자기 시간, 자기 공간만 중요하지. 조금만 다가오려고 하면 답답하다고 도망치고, 같이 있자고 하면 그거 사랑 아니고 집착이라고 뻗대고. 대체 자기 시간이 중요하면 혼자 있지 연애는 왜 하냐고!"

"섹스는 혼자 못하니까."

"뭐?"

"가까워진다 싶으면 멀어지고, 조금 멀어진다 싶으면 다시 다가오고. 네 말처럼 전형적인 회피성 애착을 가진 사람들이 그렇잖아. 그런 사람들은 자기를 돋보이게

girlfriend of three years. But Tae-hee hadn't realized until they were well into the relationship.

She cut off all contact with him for two weeks when she found out. Halfway through the two weeks, Jong-su sent her a long text saying he'd dumped the other girl. Tae-hee wasn't sure she had the magnanimity to give a liar her trust again. But time passed, and the gratefulness that he had worked up the courage to choose her over the other girl began to outweigh the disappointment that he lied to her. Eventually, she came to think of his lying as a courageous act of protecting her from anguish. Her delusion had reached heights almost as toxic as the moment she cut him out of her social media, awash with self-satisfaction that she got to cut him out before he did.

"Being in love with someone you can't trust is the worst! That asshole!" A tendon bulged on Jae-yon's neck. Perhaps the most crucial function of a friend was to rage on your behalf. Tae-hee sometimes felt as if Jae-yon was her alter-ego.

"Somebody once said that to love is to trust," Jae-yon's rant continued. "What a load of crap! Loving someone and trusting someone are completely different. Look at all those people out there who can't

하기 위해서 연애하는 경우가 많다잖아. 데이트 시장에 가장 많이 나와 있는 사람들이 그런 부류의 사람들이 야. 회피성 애착을 가진 사람에게 연애는 일종의 수단 인 거야. 연애가 자아실현의 장인 거지. 하지만 나 같은 불안정 애착이 끌리는 게 회피성 애착을 가진 사람이라 는 게 문제지. 자석처럼 서로를 끌어들이거든. 서로를 피할 방법이 없어. 너무나 큰 매력을 느끼니까."

"심리학 박사 났네. 너는 중학교 때부터 어쩜 그렇게 자기 객관화가 잘 되니? 네가 모르는 게 대체 뭐야?"

"시간이 아깝잖아. 헤어진 남자 생각하면서 후회하고 분노하기에는……."

"어쨌든 걔랑 헤어진 거 잘한 거야. 잘 된 거야."

'어쨌든'이란 말이 있어 다행이었다.

어쨌든, 밥은 먹자. 다 먹고 살자고 하는 짓이니까. 어 쨌든, 잠은 자자. 내일 출근은 해야 하니까. 어쨌든 괜찮 아진다는 말부터 꺼내놓으면, 어쨌든 괜찮아질 것 같은 기분이 들 때도 있다.

태희는 종수와 마지막으로 먹던 설렁탕이 떠올랐다. 두 개의 누덕누덕한 고기가 들어 있는 밍밍한 설렁탕이 었다. 배가 고파서 소금을 넣지도 않은 채, 입안에 계속

trust the people they love! GPS tracking! Video calls every so often to see if they're really where they say they are! People who check their boyfriend or girlfriend's social media, call logs, texts, email! Jong-su Lee is textbook avoidant attachment style. He needs alone time! He needs his space! You take one step closer, and he says you're crowding him. You want to spend time with him, and he says you're obsessed with him. If you love alone time so much, why date at all?"

"Because you can't have sex with yourself."

"What?"

"She comes closer, he steps back. She gets distant, he chases after her. Avoidant attachment style, like you said. And these types are known to date in order to show themselves off. Most people on the market fall under this category. For the avoidant attachment types, dating is a means to an end—dating as ego fulfillment. The problem is, anxious attachment types are drawn to avoidant attachment types. We attract each other like magnets. Like moth to a flame. We find each other utterly irresistible."

"Someone oughta give you a doctorate in psychology. You've been self-rationalizing like a pro since junior high. Is there anything you don't have

국물을 밀어 넣었던 것 같다. 밥알이 떠 있던 국물은 조금 더 뿌옇게 변해 있었다. 눈물은 나지 않았다.

"종수가 먼저 얘기했어."

미세먼지가 스모그처럼 짙게 끼어 눈앞이 잘 보이지 않았다. 비라도 내리면 좀 나아질 것 같았다.

"내가 먼저 헤어지자고 말한 거 아니라고."

"……."

"이종수한테 차인 거라고, 나."

3.

'불멸의 걸작'이란 제목의 기획서를 쓴 적이 있다.

사용자의 신체 사이즈에 맞게 제작되는 핸드메이드 의자에 관한 리포트였다. 제품이 얼마나 팔릴지 자신이 없었다. 워낙 고가에 마켓 사이즈도 예측하기 힘들었다. 평소 의자에 관심이 많은 것도 아니었다. 하지만 자발적으로 바빠지기로 결심한 후, 태희는 이 일을 떠 안듯 맡았다. PT 준비 전에 관련된 리포트를 꼼꼼히 읽었다. 외국계 투자회사에 다니는 친구에게 관련 애널리스트를 소개받아 업계 현황도 분석했다. 사람들에게 주목받는 100여 명의 인플루엔서들 소비 패턴과 동영상 자

figured out?"

"It's a waste of time, harboring regrets and anger toward your ex."

"Anyway, you did the right thing breaking up with him. It's better this way."

Thank god for that word: *anyway*.

Anyway, let's get something to eat. What's the point of all this if not to put food on the table? *Anyway*, let's get some sleep. Tomorrow is another workday. Just saying or hearing "Anyway, everything will be okay" was sometimes enough to make her feel okay anyway.

Tae-hee thought of her final meal with Jong-su —ox-bone soup. There were two pieces of meat floating around in bland broth. Tae-hee vaguely remembered pouring the soup into her mouth without even adding salt, she was so hungry. By the end, the rice stirred in the bowl had turned the broth a bit more opaque. But no tears.

"Jong-su was the one who said it," Tae-hee said. Particulate matter hung in the air like smog, obscuring one's vision. She wished it would rain. "I wasn't the one who broke up with him." Pause for bewilderment. "I got dumped. By Jong-su."

료도 수집했다. 자료를 읽던 밤, 태희는 문득 사람들의 소비 패턴과 지금의 연애가 무관하지 않다는 사실을 깨달았다.

요즘 물건은 값이 싸다. 김밥 한 줄에 2000원, 1만 원짜리, 5천 원짜리 티셔츠 역시 쉽게 눈에 띈다. 만 원에 양말 열 켤레를 파는 상점도 있다. 할인과 가성비는 이제 전 지구적인 시대 정신이 되었다.

패션 브랜드 '자라' 한 곳에서만 하루 100만 점의 옷이 제조된다. 통계 자료에 따르면 자라의 고객들은 평균적으로 1년에 열일곱 번 옷을 산다. 수명이 길지 않은 가구와 조명을 만드는 이케아 역시 마찬가지다. 이케아의 고객들은 평균 6개 이상의 조명 기구를 가지고 있다. 망가지는 즉시 버리거나 새로 사는 것이다.

값이 싸기 때문에 사람들은 쉽게 물건에 질린다. 사용 주기가 점점 짧아진다. 망가지지 않는 제품을 만드는 게 회사 차원에서 오히려 마이너스일 수 있다. 일부러 제품의 질을 꾸준히 낮추는 게 영업 전략이 될 수 있다는 뜻이다. 명백히 비윤리적인 행위다. 하지만 그것이 애플의 배터리 게이트처럼 집단 소송의 빌미가 되기도 한다.

3.

"Immortal Masterpiece."

That was the title of a marketing plan Tae-hee had written for a chair handmade and tailored to each individual's body size. Tae-hee wasn't sure it would sell well. It was high-end, and the market size was hard to estimate. She wasn't even all that interested in chairs. But her new resolution to keep busy forced her to take on the project. She meticulously reviewed relevant reports before putting together the presentation. She asked her friend at an investment company to put her in touch with a marketing analyst, who helped her analyze the industry status. She studied the consumption patterns of 100 social media influencers and collected related video clips. One night, while going through the material, Tae-hee realized that today's consumption patterns and dating practices had something in common.

The world is full of cheap things. Two dollars for a roll of gimbap, and ten, or even five dollars for a T-shirt. Some stores sell ten pairs of socks for ten dollars. Discounts and cost-effectiveness have become the zeitgeist.

Fashion brand ZARA alone manufactures a million

모든 현상에는 특정 비용이 발생한다. 싸구려 재료와 물건은 값싼 노동력과 노동 착취로 이어진다. 이때 환경 기준은 간단히 무시된다. 과거에는 양말에 구멍이 나면 실로 꿰매 신었다(고 한다). 신발이 닳으면 수선집에서 구두 밑창을 갈았다. 과거의 유물 같은 얘기다.

SNS 생태계에는 사람들이 넘쳐난다. 모두 제각각 매력적인 사람들이다. 그곳이 실제의 '내'가 아니라 '되고 싶은 나'를 전시하는 공간이기 때문이다. 최신 메이크업, 옷, 음악, 영화, 다양한 포토샵으로 무장한 사람들이 밀라노나 뉴욕 패션쇼 런어웨이를 걷는 모델처럼 매 순간 빠르게 등장한다. 전 세계 대도시 어디에나 있는 '자라'나 'H&M'의 문턱만큼 연애의 진입장벽은 과거에 비해 낮아졌다. 누군가에게 말을 걸거나 메시지를 보내는 게 어렵지 않은 세상이다. 잠재적 연애 대상자가 많다는 건 뭘 의미하는 걸까.

선택할 자유는 무한대로 늘어났다. 그러나 심리학에서 선택지가 많다는 건 최선이 아니다. 101개의 아이스크림 중 딱 하나를 선택해야 한다면 사람들은 극도의 혼란스러움을 느낄 것이다. 선택지가 많으면 선택을 확신할 수 없다. 사람은 스스로의 선택을 의심하는 순간,

items of clothing per day. ZARA's customers, statistics say, purchase clothes on average 17 times. The same goes for IKEA, which makes affordable but lesser quality furniture and lighting. IKEA's customers have at least six lighting fixtures at home. This means when the fixtures break, they simply throw them out or replace them.

People get sick of cheap things more quickly. They replace things faster and faster. Making robust products can turn out bad for manufacturers. In other words, making a constant effort to lower product quality can be a good sales strategy. Of course it is unethical, which could lead to class-action lawsuits like Apple's "batterygate."

Every phenomenon carries a certain cost. Low-price ingredients and goods entail cheap labor and exploitation. Environmental standards are easily ignored. There was the time when everyone darned socks(so Tae-hee was told). People took their old shoes to the cobbler's to have the soles replaced. It indeed sounds like ancient history.

Today's social media ecosystem is overpopulated. Each and every individual looks cool in their own way. Because cyberspace is not where people display "who I am," but "who I want to be," feeds of

여기가 아닌 저기를 바라본다. 태희는 이 모든 소비 현상이 지금의 연애와 무관하지 않다고 생각했다. 단지 의자 하나에 포커스를 맞출 일이 아니었다. 이 의자를 왜 사야 하는지에 대한 생각의 전환이 필요했다.

고장 나지 않는 제품이 아니라, 고쳐 쓰고 싶은 제품을 만들 필요가 있었다. 완벽한 사람을 만나는 게 아니라, 노력하고 싶은 사람을 만나야 한다. 상대가 바뀌길 바라는 게 아니라, 나 자신의 생각을 바꿀 만큼 가치 있는 상대를 만나는 일 말이다. 태희에게는 종수가 그런 사람이었는지에 대한 믿음이 없었다.

그날, 태희는 책상에 앉아 노트북이 아닌 종이를 펼쳤다. 몇 년 만에 연필을 깎았다. 작은 칼로 연필을 깎다가, 이 연필 한 자루를 다 사용하려면 얼마나 걸릴까 헤아렸다. 몽당연필이란 단어가 완전히 사라지게 될 날은 언제쯤일까. 그 밤 태희는 종이 위에 자신이 생각한 글을 정리했다.

물건값이 싸다.

너무 싸서 쉽게 질린다.

질리면 즉시 바꾼다.

people armed with new makeup trends, fashion, music, film, and marvelous photoshop skills, swiftly appear on the screen like models on a runway in Milan or New York. Just like anyone can visit ZARA or H&M stores wherever they go, today's dating has lower barriers to entry than ever before. It is so easy to talk to, or send a message to a stranger these days. Then, what can this upsurge of potential dating partners imply?

Accessible options have increased to infinity. But psychology propounds that having more options may not be a good thing. If you had to choose just one among 101 different ice cream flavors, you'd feel extremely conflicted. When you have too many options, you can't be sure you made the right choice, and the moment doubting creeps in, you start looking over the fence for greener pastures.

Tae-hee believed all of these consumption phenomena were somehow related to the dating practices of this era. To sell the chair, she needed something more than just a chair: a paradigm shift on why one should ever buy a keeper.

This called for products that made you want to go to the trouble of fixing it, not one so hardy it never broke. What people needed wasn't the per-

고쳐 쓰지 않고 바꿔 입는 옷이나 구두처럼 사람을 바꾼다.

바꿀 수 있을 때 언제든 바꾸겠다는 의지의 표명, 그 것이 '썸'이다.

빨리 선택하면 손해라는 생각은 언제부터 사람들의 마음을 파고들었을까. 얻는 것보다 잃는 걸 훨씬 더 힘들 어하는 우리의 마음은 언제부터 선택과 맞부딪쳤을까.

태희는 자신이 쓴 기획서를 바라봤다. 며칠을 매달려 서 쓴 기획서가 결국은 종수에게 하고 싶은 말이었다.

'불멸의 걸작'이라는 제목의 폰트가 붉게 반짝거리고 있었다.

불멸이 꼭 불면처럼 보였다.

4.

"헤어지고 다시 만나는 커플이 몇 퍼센트인 줄 알아?"

공원을 걷던 재연이 태희에게 커다란 호밀빵 샌드위 치를 건네주며 말했다. 인디 음악 축제가 벌어지는 공 원 여기저기에 움직이는 대형 무대가 설치되어 있었다.

fect someone, but someone who made them want to change; it wasn't about waiting for the partner to change, but finding someone who was worth changing your attitude for. But Tae-hee wasn't sure if Jong-su was that certain someone.

That day, at her desk, Tae-hee opened a notebook instead of her laptop. She sharpened a pencil, which she hadn't done in years. She wondered, holding a small box cutter in her hand, *How many years would it take to use up this one pencil?* When would the word "pencil stub" fade into history? That night, Tae-hee jotted down her thoughts in the notebook.

Things are cheap.

So cheap that people get bored with them easily.

When bored, they immediately replace the items with new ones.

They don't mend things, but get new clothes and shoes, as they do with people.

Repairing is not an option. As with clothes and shoes, they replace people.

Assigning no labels and keeping it terminable whenever—the essence of having a "thing" with someone.

무대 주위로 철제 펜스가 쳐 있었다. 공연 시작 전인데
도 빈 의자에 앉아 있는 몇 명의 사람들이 보였다.

"헤어지고도 다시 만나는 커플이 82퍼센트래."

"82퍼센트가 서로를 스토킹하고 있었단 소리네."

태희는 의자 맨 끝에 앉아 있는 남녀를 바라보다가
재연에게 지나가듯 말했다. 남녀는 서로에게 집중하느
라 주위를 살피지 못하고 있었다. 목소리가 들리지 않
아도, 몸짓 하나로 정황을 파악할 수 있는 경우가 있다.
싸우는 남녀의 파장은 몇십 미터 밖에서도 단박에 알
수 있었다.

"내 주위를 봐도 헤어져서 두 달을 못 넘기고 다시 만
나더라. 의지력이 없어진 건가?"

"참을 필요가 없어진 거지."

"눈에 빤히 보여서?"

"다이어트할 거면 과자를 아예 사놓으면 안 되는 거
야. 눈에 보이는 곳에 과자 사놓고 의지력 시험을 왜
해?"

"태희 너, 이종수 스토킹하니?"

"안 하는 사람도 있니? 걔도 하고 있을걸?"

"헤어졌던 사람이 다시 만나서 잘 될 확률은 얼마나

When did the mentality of "the sooner we choose the more we lose" start to infiltrate our minds? When did our minds, far more vulnerable to what we lose than what we gain, begin to conflict with our choice?

Tae-hee looked at the project plan she wrote. The report that she'd been tied up with for days and nights turned out to be what she had wanted to say to Jong-su.

Immortal Masterpiece. The title in red glared back at her.

"Immortal" was beginning to look like "insomniac."

4.

"Wanna know the percentage of couples who break up and get back together again?" Jae-yon asked, handing Tae-hee a large rye sandwich as they made their way through the park. Big move-able stages were set up all across the park where an indie music festival was being held. Chain-linked fences enclosed the stages. Seats were starting to fill up long before the concert was to begin.

"Eighty-two."

"So eighty-two percent break up and stalk their

되게?"

재연이 스피드 퀴즈를 내듯 태희를 바라보며 빠르게
물었다.

"3퍼센트! 〈연애의 온도〉에 나오잖아."

"영화 봤어?"

"97퍼센트는 만나도 또 헤어진다는 얘기지. 옛날에
헤어졌던 똑같은 이유로. 재연이 너도 그랬잖아. 안 그
래?"

"우리 서로에게 너무 잔인하다!"

"정확한 거지."

"솔직히 나는 헤어지는 그 순간까지도 우리가 정말
헤어지는 건지 확신이 안 들더라. 이러다가 또 만나는
거 아냐? 이런 생각도 들면서 묘하게 안심도 되고. 아
진짜 짜증 난다."

지금의 연애가 과거에 비해 짜증스러워진 건 확실하
다.

끝날 때까지는 끝난 게 아니기 때문이다. 전설적인 야
구 선수 '요기 베라'가 했다는 이 말은 연애에도 적용된
다. 9회 말 끝나도 10회 초가 기다리고 있다. 승부가 나
지 않은 채 연장전이 끝없이 이어질 것 같은 예감으로

exes," Tae-hee said in passing as she glanced over at the man and woman sitting at the opposite end of the row of seats. The couple was too focused on each other to notice their surroundings. All it takes is one gesture to figure out what's going on between two people, even if you're not within ear-shot. The vibe emanating from a couple arguing can be detected from dozens of yards away.

"Everyone I know gets back together within two months after they break up. Kids these days have no willpower."

"Kids these days have no need for willpower."

"Because they know they'll get back together anyway?"

"If you're going on a diet, you don't pick up snacks at the store. Why leave snacks lying around in plain view and test your willpower?"

"Tae-hee. Are you stalking Jong-su?"

"Who doesn't stalk their ex? I'll bet he's doing it, too."

"Wanna know the percentage of couples who get back together who make it?" The question rushed out of Jae-yon too fast for Tae-hee to stop her.

"Three percent! It was in *Very Ordinary Couple*."

"Dang! You saw that movie, too?"

가득한 10회 말도 있다. 모두 SNS 때문이다.

이별은 과거에도 힘들었지만 점점 더 힘들어지고 있다. 기술이 발달할 미래의 이별은 너무나 어려워서 오히려 쉬워질지도 모른다.

〈전처가 옆방에 산다〉는 제목의 드라마를 본 적이 있다. 〈구여친 클럽〉이란 드라마 제목을 봤을 때, 이젠 헤어진 전남편과 다시 연애하게 된다는 이야기가 새롭지 않다는 걸 깨달았다. 전처와 구여친과 구남친이 수시로 출몰하는 시대에 살고 있으므로 우리에겐 과거를 잊을 자유가 없다.

재연의 말처럼 꼭 개인의 의지력 문제가 아니었다. 초연결 사회에서 사라지거나 잊히는 건 권력이었다. 울리는 전화를 받지 않아도 되는 게 특권인 것처럼 말이다.

종수를 SNS 친구 목록에서 삭제했다고 해서, 그를 보지 않을 수 있는 게 아니었다. 헤어진 연인과 나, 이 둘 모두를 아는 친구들이 존재할 때, 상황은 더 복잡했다. 가령 거대한 단체 카톡방이 만들어지고 불시에 두 사람을 초대한 친구가 생길 수 있기 때문이다. 원치 않아도 마주치게 되는 순간 때문에 감정은 점점 울창한 숲처럼 자란다. 그러므로 이제는 헤어짐을 친구들에게도 공표

"That means 97 percent of people who get back together break up again," said Tae-hee. "For the same reason they broke up the first time. That happened to you, remember?"

"We know each other too well for our own good."

"We understand each other too accurately."

"Honestly, even as we were breaking up, I wasn't sure we were really breaking up. I was oddly comforted by the thought that we would probably end up together again. Gah! I hate this," cried Jae-yon.

Dating has indisputably gotten more annoying in recent years. In the words of the legendary baseball player Yogi Berra, "It ain't over till it's over." This applies to dating as well. At the bottom of the ninth, there's still the possibility of the tenth. You sometimes get to the bottom of the tenth, and find yourself overcome with a sense of dread that the overtime will drag on forever. All because of social media.

If breaking up was hard in the past, it's getting even harder. Maybe technological advancements will make breakups so impossible in the future it'll become paradoxically easy.

Tae-hee once saw a TV show called *My Ex Lives Next Door*. And she saw the show title *Ex-Girlfriend*

해야 한다. 이별을 통보하긴 쉬워졌지만 이별을 유지하기 위해 우리가 해야 할 일이 너무나 많아졌다.

'알 수도 있는 사람'이라는 소셜 네트워크 알고리즘을 통해 헤어진 연인의 소식을 알게 되는 세상을, 사라지지 않고 쌓이기만 하는 지금의 세계를, 사람들은 과연 예측했을까. 종수의 새 여자 친구의 얼굴을 보던 날, 태희는 생각했다.

많이 닮아 있었다.
스마트폰 속 종수의 옛 여자친구와.

5.
unfriend.
친구 목록에서 삭제한다는 뜻의 이 동사는 '옥스퍼드 사전'이 2009년의 단어로 선정했다. 다양한 소셜 네트워크에 등록된 친구들 가운데 더 이상 연결을 원하지 않는 사람을 지우는 것을 뜻하는 이 단어가 의미하는 건 '삭제'다.

태희는 종수와 헤어진 밤, 바로 자신의 계정을 비활성화시켰다. 스마트폰 속 바탕화면에 있는 특정 앱도 모

Club, she learned that the "getting back together with an ex-husband" plotline was nothing new. In an age where every corner you turn there's your ex-wife, ex-girlfriend, ex-boyfriend, you don't have the freedom to leave the past behind you.

Was Jae-yon right? Was it all just a matter of individual willpower? In a hyper-connected society, disappearing or being forgotten required power. Only the privileged got to screen calls.

Blocking Jong-su on social media didn't mean Tae-hee never had to see him again. There was the matter of mutual friends. Someone could make a huge group chatroom on KakaoTalk and invite both of them. The incidents of unwanted virtual run-ins unleashed emotions that ran wild and grew like an impenetrable jungle. So breaking up meant sending out a newsletter to all mutual friends. *Dumping* someone was easier now but it took serious work to *stay broken up*.

Who would have imagined, thought Tae-hee, *a world where you hear about your ex through an algorithm called "People You May Know?" A world where everything is saved, nothing lost?* Tae-hee wondered on the day she saw Jong-su's new girlfriend's face on the Internet.

두 지웠다. 문제는 채 24시간도 되지 않아 다시 계정을 활성화하고 앱도 복구했다는 것이다.

댄 에리얼리는 다양한 사고 실험을 통해 인간이 얼마나 비이성적인지 연구한 행동경제학자다. 그가 유독 인간의 '고통'이나 '불합리성'에 주목했던 건 청소년 시절 겪었던 화재 사고 때문이었다. 화상 치료를 하며 보낸 청춘이 그에게 어떤 영향을 끼쳤는지 모른다. 그러나 흥미로운 건 그의 사고 실험 중에는 유독 인간이 고전 경제학이 말하는 합리적 소비 주체가 아닌, 얼마나 불완전하며 감정적인지 보여주는 연구가 많다는 것이다. '거짓말하는 착한 사람들'이라는 그의 책 제목처럼 기회만 되면 사람이 얼마나 쉽게 타인을 속이고, 자신을 기만하는지를 보여주는 연구들 말이다.

데이팅 앱에 관한 연구 결과도 그렇다.

사람들이 소셜 미디어에서 데이트 상대를 찾는 과정에 쓰는 시간은 주당 12시간이다. 하지만 실제 만남에 사람들이 쓰는 시간은 1.8시간이었다. 비율로 따지면 6:1이다. 심리를 공부한 경제학자가 주목한 건 SNS 데이트 시장의 경제적 비효율성이었다. 그것이 친구와 딱 1시간 대화하기 위해 자동차로 왕복 6시간 걸리는 바

A spitting image.

Of a picture of Jong-su' ex Tae-hee once found on his phone.

5.

unfriend

v. to remove(someone) from a list of friends or contacts on a social networking website.

This verb was selected as Oxford Dictionary's Word of the Year 2009. The word is defined as the act of disconnecting from a person you don't want to have on the list of "friends" of various social networking sites. It means *delete*.

On the very night Tae-hee broke up with Jong-su, she deactivated her social media accounts. And deleted some of the apps from her phone. The problem was, it took her less than 24 hours to re-activate the accounts and reinstall the apps.

Dan Ariely is a behavioral economist who has conducted various thought experiments on how ir-rational humans can be. His study mainly focused on humans' pain and irrationality, which was in-spired by the fire that left him with a serious burn injury when he was a teenager. It is unclear how his days of youth spent in burn treatments influ-

닻가를 찾는 것과 다를 바가 없기 때문이다. 하지만 사람은 녹을 줄 알면서도 눈사람을 만든다. 다시 복구할 걸 알면서도 소셜 네트워크 관련 앱을 계속 지운다. 세일 중이라거나 나중에 먹겠다는 핑계를 대며, 다이어트 중에 초콜릿과 아이스크림을 냉장고에 넣어두며 실패를 자초한다.

태희 역시 헤어진 연인들의 소셜 네트워크 계정을 살펴보는 데 자신이 얼마만큼의 시간을 쓰는지 계산한 적이 있었다. 막연히 많은 시간을 허비하고 있다가 아니라, 헤어진 후 감량한 몸무게처럼 구체적인 숫자가 필요했다. 태희가 보기에 이런 일의 가장 큰 문제는 한 사람을 관찰하기 위해 수많은 사람의 계정을 넘나들어야 한다는 것이었다.

초연결 사회라는 말은 사회학 서적이나 IT 기사가 아니라, 헤어진 옛 애인을 스토킹하는 순간, 절감하게 된다. 이때 구글은 익사 당한 시체들로 널린 광대한 블랙홀로 변한다.

하루 평균 5.8시간. 태희가 헤어진 연인의 상태를 확인하기 위해 사용하고 있는 시간이었다. 회사에 있는 시간을 빼면, 집에서, 길에서, 지하철에서, 클라이언트

enced his life. Still, what's interesting is that many of his thought experiments, unlike the traditional economic principle of humans as rational consumers, are about how irrational and emotional we humans are. Just as the title of his book—*The Honest Truth about Dishonesty*—suggests, his studies mainly focus on how humans deceive other people and themselves.

Ariely also studied dating apps. He discovered people spend about 12 hours a week finding a date on social media, and only 1.8 hour on the actual date. The ratio is 6 to 1. Standing at the point where economics meets psychology, the economist paid attention to the underlying inefficiency of the online dating market: finding a date online is no different than taking a six-hour round-trip to the beach just to have a one-hour conversation with a friend. But you build a snowman, knowing it will melt. People delete social media apps, knowing they will reinstall them later. People on diets make excuses—*Sweets* are on sale now! I'm just saving them for some time later!—for stocking up on blocks of chocolate and ice cream in their fridge, only to woo their own failure.

The other day, Tae-hee calculated how much

를 기다리는 미팅룸에서도, 그녀는 계속 상대의 SNS를 분석했다. 낮에는 그럭저럭 일하며 버텼다. 하지만 밤이 되면 낮 동안 쓴 의지력이 전부 고갈돼 그녀를 괴롭혔다.

물론 모든 일에 그림자만 있는 건 아니다. 종수의 글이나 사진에 '좋아요'를 누르는 사람, 댓글을 단 사람, 태그되어 있는 사람들과 그 사람들의 계정 일부에 남아 있는 다양한 흔적은 태희에게 동기를 부여했다. 특히 올렸다가 바로 사라지는 사진과 링크됐다가 바로 삭제되는 링크에 관해서라면 더 그랬다. 숨기고 싶은 게 많은 사람의 비밀 정원을 엿보는 기분이 들었기 때문이다.

어느 날엔 거실 소파 의자에 앉아 홍차를 홀짝이며 창밖의 살인사건을 추리하는 '미스 마플 여사'라도 된 것 같았다. 하지만 서서히 밝아지는 창문을 바라보다가, 출근길 지하철에서 내려야 할 역을 놓치는 해프닝을 반복했다. 서울에 사는데도 마치 뉴욕에 사는 사람처럼 시차가 어긋나기 시작했다. 하지만 태희는 이종수의 과거를 재구성하는 일을 멈출 수 없었다. 그녀의 욕망은 오타쿠적 기질과 합체돼 점점 더 학구적인 성격을 띠기 시작했다.

time she spent on social media accounts of her ex-boyfriends. She needed more than the vague assumption that she was wasting a lot of time on doing it. What she needed was concrete numbers like the weight she lost after the breakup. The biggest problem, it seemed to her, was that one had to visit so many accounts of other people, just to monitor the one person that mattered.

You can read about "hyperconnectivity" in a social science book or an IT article, but nothing makes the concept real for you like spying on your ex online. That is the moment when Google turns into a vast black hole that sucks in dead husks of ex-lover stalkers.

An average of 5.8 hours per day. That was how long she spent checking the status of her ex-boyfriend. Every moment she was not working, she analyzed his social media feeds —at home, walking down the street, on the subway, or even in the meeting room waiting for a client. In the daytime, she managed to keep herself in check at the office. But at night, the willpower she had depleted during the day plunged her right back into it.

All was not gloom and self-hate, however. Those who "liked" Jong-su's posts, who left comments,

태희에게 전 남친 증후군이란 단어가 떠오른 건 그때였다. 태희는 이종수와 관련된 정보들에서 행간을 읽고, 그것이 의미하는 바를 끌어내 찢긴 책의 클라이맥스의 일부를 읽어 내려갔다.

사람들은 흔히 자신이 원하는 것을 알고 있다고 착각한다. 하지만 대개의 사람은 자신이 원하는 것이 무엇인지 구체적으로 모른다. 적어도 다른 사람들이 '그것'을 원하기 전까지는 말이다. 그러므로 욕망은 얼마든지 설계할 수 있다. 조작이나 설계가 힘든 건 오히려 욕망하지 않는 것이 무엇이냐 하는 것이다.

"가장 탁월한 카피라이터는 그 사람이 하고 싶은 말이 아니라 결코 하고 싶지 않은 말을 알아내는 법이지."

입사하고 나서 얼마 후, 선배가 회의에서 했던 말을 태희는 아직 기억했다. 그 사람의 본질은 절대 말하고 싶어 하지 않는 그것에 있다. 이종수가 올렸다가 지워버린 사진들, 일부러 삭제한 링크와 삭제한 댓글이야말로, 그가 남에게 보여주고 싶지 않은 자신의 진짜 모습일 것이다. 헤어지고 나서야, 태희는 종수에 대해 더 많은 걸 알게 됐다. 이전에는 한 번도 생각해보지 않은 방법으로 그를 검색한 탓이다. 헤어진 연인이 일종의 범

who were tagged in his photos, and other traces of him left on parts of other people's accounts gave her a high and motivated her to keep on clicking. Particularly when it came to the photos he posted and took down immediately, and the links posted only for a couple of minutes before they were deleted, she felt like she was peeping into the secret garden of the one who wanted to keep so many things to himself.

One day, Tae-hee felt as if she had become some sort of Miss Marple sitting on the sofa in the living room, sipping tea and trying to get the full picture of the murder case that happened outside her window. She would stare out the window and watch as it grew lighter outside, which eventually led to her spacing out on the subway and missing her stop on the way to work. She lived in Seoul, but her clock was ticking in a different time zone as if she were in New York. But Tae-hee couldn't stop reconstructing the past of Jong-su Lee. Her desire, combined with her nerdiness, started to take on a scholarly vibe.

It was right then that the term "ex-boyfriend syndrome" popped up in her head. She read between the feeds containing any information about

죄자처럼 느껴지는 것도 검색 때문이었다.

단지 그의 이메일과 핸드폰 번호, 학교, 학번, 주민등록증 번호만으로도 생각지 못한 정보가 쏟아졌다. 9년 전 한 중고 사이트에서 종수가 팔기 위해 내놓은 노트북과 구찌 구두, 스노보드를 발견한 순간, 태희는 종수의 청춘이 자신의 생각과 다를 수 있음을 직감했다. 종수의 여자 친구로 보이는 여자가 과거에 사용하던 SNS 계정 속에서, 검은색 고양이를 안고 있는 그의 사진을 발견했을 때 그녀의 예감은 확신이 됐다.

속옷 차림의 그는 부엌 의자에 다리를 꼬고 앉아 잇몸을 드러낸 채 웃고 있었다. 태희의 눈에 핑크빛 레이스가 잔뜩 달린 커튼이 눈에 띄었다. 블랙과 화이트를 지향하는 이종수의 취향과는 거리가 너무 먼 디자인이었다. 부엌 위, 컵 선반에 놓여 있는 나란한 두 개의 머그잔에서 태희는 이들의 동거 흔적을 발견했다. 손 걸이 모양과 크기가 전혀 다른 머그잔은 직접 만든 공예품 같았다. 태희는 사진 밑에 적혀 있는 댓글 하나를 발견했다.

댓글에는 고양이의 이름처럼 보이는 명사 하나가 적혀 있었다.

Jong-su Lee, and drew certain meanings from them to piece together what was written in the missing pages of the book's climax.

People tend to think they know what they want. But most of them do not know exactly what they want. At least not until other people want the thing. Desires can be designed. What's difficult to design or manipulate is the thing that people do not desire.

"The best copywriters are those who pinpoint not what people want to say, but what they would never say."

Tae-hee remembered what her senior had said at a meeting when she was a newcomer at the company. The true nature of a person lies in the thing that the person would never say out loud. The photos deleted right away and the links and comments deliberately removed were the very things that spoke volumes of who he really was, a part of himself he didn't want others to see. It was not until she broke up with him that she learned more things about him, thanks to the new search skill she'd never thought of before. After all the investigating, Tae-hee was starting to perceive her ex-boyfriend as a criminal.

His e-mail address, phone number, college, year

누가 지었든 고양이에게 '바둑이'라는 강아지 이름을 붙여놓고 좋아했을 이 커플의 한때가 떠올랐다. 칼에 베인 듯 마음이 아팠다. 하지만 동시에 기이한 쾌감이 밀려왔다. 종수에 대해 알아갈수록 상황을 통제하고 있다는 생각이 들었다.

그의 잠재적 연애 대상자들의 목록은 점점 더 늘어났다. 데이터 마이닝이 시작된 지 5일 만에, 태희는 이종수의 옛날 휴대폰 번호를 알아냈다. 그의 숨겨진 과거가 그녀 앞에 펼쳐졌다. 그것은 찢어진 페이지로,

가령 그의 새 여자 친구에 관한 이야기 같은 게 그랬다.

6.

오전 8시 11분, 한남대로 위에 서 있는 택시 안에서 태희는 벗겨지기 시작한 젤 네일을 무의식적으로 뜯어 냈다. 처음에는 손톱 물어뜯는 걸 방지하기 위해 시작한 네일 손질이었다. 하지만 이젠 손톱이 상하는 줄 알면서도, 금이 가거나 깨진 매니큐어 조각을 습관처럼 긁어내고 있었다.

창문에 비친 태희의 얼굴 위에 미술관 설치 작품처럼

of matriculation, and resident registration number gave her access to a whole lot of information about him she'd never expected to find before. When she found out about a laptop, a pair of Gucci shoes, and a snowboard that he posted on a second-hand goods website nine years ago, it occurred to her that the days of Jong-su's youth might have been different from what she had thought. From an old social media account of a girl who seemed like Jong-su's then girlfriend, Tae-hee found a photo of him holding a black cat, which turned her hunch into reality.

Jong-su in his underwear, a wide toothy grin on his face, was sitting in a kitchen chair with his legs crossed. Tae-hee's eyes reached the curtain with pink lace trimmings behind him. It was far from his taste, who always insisted on black and white. Two mugs placed side by side on the cupboard shelf told her that they were living together. The handles of the two mugs were totally different in shape and size, which indicated they were handcrafted. Tae-hee found a comment left on the photo.

A noun. Probably the cat's name.

Him and her and their cat, whosever idea it was to name it "Snoopy," and their happy days together

물이 흐르고 있었다. 습관처럼 창문을 열기 전, 태희는 미세먼지 앱을 작동시켰다. 비가 내리고 있는데도 미세먼지 수치가 나빴다. 담배에 찌든 택시 시트에서 습기와 함께 퀴퀴한 냄새가 올라왔다. 창을 열어도 열지 않아도 꿉꿉하긴 마찬가지였다.

고백하면, 종수와 헤어진 후 상황이 그리 나빠지는 않았다. 확실히 미워할 대상이 생기자 회사의 다른 사람들이 덜 미워지기도 했다. 잘 살고 있을 이종수를 생각하며, 자기계발의 의지를 불태울 수 있는 건 이별의 장점이었다. 확실히 덜 자고, 더 많이 수영장 트랙을 돌았다. 몸무게가 3.6킬로그램 빠졌다. 맞지 않던 스키니 진이 예쁘게 맞았다. 단지 그런 자신의 모습을 보여주고, 자랑하고 싶은 게 이종수라는 게 문제였다.

"헤어졌는데 다시 만나고 싶었던 남친 있었어?"

태희가 재연에게 물었다.

최대한 건조하게 물어야 최소한 솔직한 답이 나올 것 같았다. 그런데 재연의 목소리가 튀어 오르듯 높아졌다.

"설마! 태희 너, 이종수 다시 만난 거야?"

"아니."

"절대 만나지 마! 헤어진 전 남친 다시 만나는 거, 그거

—it cut Tae-hee like a knife. But at the same time, a weird pleasure welled up in her. The more she dug up about Jong-su, the more she felt like she was in control of the situation.

The list of his possible dating partners grew longer and longer. On the fifth day of her data-mining, she found out his old phone number. His hidden past opened up before her eyes. Like pages previously torn out.

On one of those pages was his ex-then-current-again-girlfriend.

6.

08:11. In a cab stuck on Hannam Motorway, Tae-hee was unconsciously peeling the gel polish off her nails. She'd started getting her nails done to quit the habit of biting them, but the biting turned to peeling or scratching off the cracked or chipped polish, knowing it was bad for her nails.

Water streamed down the reflection of her face on the window. It looked like an installation piece. Before rolling the window down as usual, Tae-hee tapped on the Air Quality Index App on her phone. The number was high even though it was raining.

하는 거 아냐. 영혼까지 너덜너덜해지는 일이라니까."

재연은 태희의 말을 믿지 않는 눈치였다.

"아니라니까 그러네."

"나 같은 경우는 헤어지고 나면 최소한 서너 달은 후회했어. 헤어지면 나쁜 건 지워지고 좋았던 것만 생각나잖아. 그게 이별의 신박한 능력이잖아. 태희 너도 그럴 거야. 그러니까 내 말은 지금이 고비니까 절대 만나거나 전화하면 안 된다는 거야."

"안 만났다니까!"

"그랬겠지. 네가 헤어진 남자친구 프로필 사진에 '좋아요'를 누른 건 실수였겠지. 그건 나도 알아."

사람은 실수한다. 문제는 같은 실수를 반복하는 것이다. 누가 먼저 헤어지자고 말했는지는 중요하지 않다. 중요한 건 만났다는 것이고, 다시 헤어졌다는 것이며, 또다시 실패했다는 것이다.

평소보다 서너 배는 많은 생각이 머릿속을 탱크처럼 뭉개며 지나갔다. 명상 전문가들은 머릿속 수많은 생각이 진짜 나, 진정한 자아가 아니라고 강조했다. 그들은 그것이 그저 감정들의 시끄러운 목소리일 뿐이라고 주장했다. 하지만 가슴 속의 '참 자아'가 명상 동영상을 틀

The humidity was really brining out the dank, musty smell of the cab seat infused with the smell of cigarettes. It was going to be muggy whether she opened the window or not.

To be frank, Tae-hee was doing okay after the breakup. Her anger focused on one person, her resentment toward her coworkers abated. The benefit of breaking up was that she could fan the flames of her self-improvement fanaticism by picturing Jong-su doing just fine without her. She slept less and swam more. She lost 3.6 kilograms. She slimmed into the cute pair of skinny jeans that didn't fit before. Only problem was, Jong-su was the one she wanted to show herself off to.

"Was there ever a time when you broke up with someone and wanted to get back together with him?" Tae-hee asked Jaeyon in her most nonchalant voice so as to elicit an honest response. Alas, it didn't work.

"YOU! You met up with Jong-su, didn't you?"

"No."

"Do not meet up with him! Never get together with an ex-boyfriend. It leaves your soul in tatters!" Jae-yon seemed convinced Tae-hee was lying.

"I didn't see him."

어놓고 눈을 감거나, 주말 명상 코스 등록으로 찾아질 것 같지 않았다. 참선 수업 내내 졸기만 했던 태희에겐 명상도, 호흡도, 도움이 되지 않긴 마찬가지였다.

헤어진 그 사람을 잊지 못하는 자신이 부끄럽다. 부끄러움을 잊기 위해 술을 마신다. 자꾸 술을 마시는 자신이 부끄러워서, 잊기 위해 다시 술을 마신다. 어느 알코올 중독자의 고백처럼 느껴졌지만, 그게 바로 자신에게 벌어진 일이었다. 그럴듯한 변명이라도 찾고 싶어졌다. 그녀는 '수입 맥주 4캔에 만 원'이라고 적힌 편의점 세일 문구 때문이라고 소리치고 싶은 마음을 억눌렀다.

헤어진 여자친구를 5년 만에 '다시' 만났다면 그건 5년 동안 잊지 못했다는 뜻일까, 5년 만에 다시 사랑에 빠졌다는 뜻일까.

태희는 택시 창문에 비친 자신의 얼굴을 보며 되뇌었다. 주먹을 꽉 쥐자 뾰족한 손톱이 손바닥을 파고들었다. 기사가 틀어놓은 라디오에선 디제이가 오프닝 멘트를 하고 있었다.

– 희극 작가 아리스토파네스가 이렇게 말했습니다. 우리는 자신을 완성하기 위해 타인을 필요로 한다. 어

"For me, the regret lasts three to four months after the breakup. You split up, and the bad stuff gets wiped from your memories and you only remember the good times. That's the magic of breaking up. It's happening to you, too. What I'm saying is, this is a crucial period when you cannot, no matter what, see him or call him."

"I said I didn't see him!"

"I believe you. I believe that your finger slipped and hit "Like" on your ex-boyfriend's new Facebook profile pic. I understand."

People made mistakes. Problem was, some people repeated the same mistakes. It wasn't important who broke up with whom the second time around. The point was: she got back together with him, broke up with him again, and thus failed again.

About three, four times the volume of her usual thoughts jammed through her head like a tank, leveling everything in its wake. Meditation experts claimed at that the numerous thoughts running through one's head were not one's true self, or "the real me." They were only clamors of myriad emotions. Listening to a meditation tape with her eyes closed or going on a weekend meditation retreat, however, wasn't going to let "the real Tae-hee"

떤가요, 그런 사람이 있나요, 당신에게는?

종수의 헤어진 후, 자꾸 떠오르는 노래가 있었다. 그
와 함께 들었던 기억 같은 건 없다. 하지만 계속 그 노래
가 몸에서 떠나지 않았다. 어쩌면 그것이 무의식이 알
려주려는 진짜 진실인지도 모른다. 진심과 다른 진실.
"이봐, 아가씨!"
택시 문을 열었다. 택시 기사가 뒤돌아 바라보며 태희
에게 소리쳤다.
"대체 무슨 짓이에요?"
빗방울이 그녀의 뺨을 후려치듯 들이쳤다.

7.
한 사람이 누군가를 향해 던졌던 물컵 하나가 온 가
족을 범죄자로 만들 수 있다. 사소해 보이는 작은 균열
이 건물을 무너뜨릴 수 있다. 회사를 그만두면, 회사를
차리고 싶다고 생각했다. 입사하고 나서야 자신의 꿈이
퇴사가 된 사람들처럼 돌이킬 수 없는 감정에 빠져들었
다고 생각했다. 스스로를 보호하기 위해 언제나 노력했
는데 종수를 아프게 하고 싶다는 욕망이 자신을 보호하

surface from deep within. Meditation and breathing exercises weren't useful either for Tae-hee who slept through her Buddhist meditation class.

You are ashamed of yourself because you can't get over him. You drink to get over the shame. You drink more to get over the shame of drinking. What sounds like every alcoholic's story was exactly what happened to Tae-hee. She wished she had a more legitimate excuse for the binge drinking. She wanted to shout, IMPORT BEER: 4 CANS FOR 10,000 WON! How do you say no to that sign calling out to you at the convenience store?

If a guy gets back together with someone he broke up with five years ago, does that mean they fell back in love after five years? Or was he thinking of her for five years? Tae-hee asked, staring at her reflection. Her nails dug into her palms as she clenched her fists. On the radio, the DJ was opening a show with this food for thought: *Ancient Greek playwright Aristophanes once said, "To become whole, we need to find our other half." What are your thoughts? Do you have someone, who makes you whole?*

One song kept playing over and over again in Tae-hee's head after she broke up with Jong-su. She had no memories of the two of them listening

고 싶다는 본능보다 점점 더 강해졌다.

"부러진 게 오른쪽이 아닌 건 그나마 다행이네."

재연이 깁스한 태희의 다리를 바라보며 말했다.

"택시 기사한테는 뭐라고 그런 거야?"

"저 돈 없어요!"

"대단하다, 너."

"안 막히면 15분이면 가는 거리인데, 택시비 5만 원이 말이 돼?"

"그렇다고 달리는 택시에서 뛰어내려? 분노조절 장애야? 격분 증후군 뭐 그런 거니?"

"소진 증후군이야. 수면 장애, 소화 장애, 위장 장애, 기분 장애……."

태희의 깁스 위에는 회사 사람들이 적어놓은 낙서가 가득했다. 그날 밤, 태희는 깁스 위에 그려져 있던 하트의 숫자를 세며, 잠깐 기분이 좋아지기도 했다. 그녀에게 지금의 자신은 너무 낯설었다. 거울을 봐도 도무지 자신 같지가 않았다. '네가 이럴 줄 몰랐어!'라는 말은 종수가 아닌 자신에게 되묻고 싶은 질문이었다.

"그 번호는 뭐야?"

재연이 유별나게 크게 적혀 있는 스마트폰 번호 하나

to the song together. But the song continued to echo through her body. Perhaps her unconscious was trying to communicate to her a real fact—fact, as distinct from faith.

"Hey, lady!" The cab driver turned and yelled at Tae-hee as she opened the cab door. "What the hell?"

Raindrops kept slapping her in the face.

7.

One person throwing a cup at another person can turn an entire family into a band of criminals. One small crack in the wall can demolish a building. Quitting a job could make someone want to build a whole industry. Like people whose ambition in life became retirement, but only after they were hired, Tae-hee told herself that she had been sucked into an impulse she couldn't crawl out of. Despite her vigilant efforts to protect herself, her need to make Jong-su suffer overpowered her instinct for self-preservation.

"At least you didn't break the right side," said Jae-yon, looking down at Tae-hee's leg in a cast.

"What did you say to the cab driver?"

"I'm broke!"

를 가리켰다.

"연락하라는 거 아니겠어?"

"그사이 헤어지고 다른 사람 만난 거야?"

"헤어지다니?"

"이종수 다시 만났잖아."

"정말 그렇게 생각해?"

"너 본 지 13년이 넘었어. 속는 척하는 것도, 네 거짓말 들어주기도 쉽지만은 않아."

재연이 혀를 차며 태희를 바라봤다.

태희도 알고 있었다. 과거 자신 때문에 헤어졌던 옛 여자를 다시 만났다는 게, 헤어진 그 남자를 다시 만날 이유가 되진 않는다. 그것이 비합리적이고 감정적인 선택인지 모르는 게 아니다. 달리는 택시에서 문을 열고 내리면 다리가 부러질 거란 걸 모르는 사람은 없다. 하지만 이런 얘기라면 가능할 것이다. 한 시간 가까이 꽉 막힌 한남대로에서 택시가 그 순간 움직일 거라고 예상하지 못했을 뿐이라고. 그렇다고 부러진 다리가 도로 붙는 건 아니지만.

세상의 많은 영화들이 공항 장면으로 끝난다. 새로운 시작을 알리는 엔딩 씬에는 하늘을 향해 이륙하는 비행

"Well done, you."

"It's a fifteen-minute drive without traffic. The meter read 50,000 won!"

"So you jumped out of a moving cab, did ya? What is it—anger management issues? Post-traumatic embitterment disorder?"

"Burnout syndrome. Sleep disorder. Indigestion. Ulcer. Mood disorder."

Coworkers had filled Tae-hee's cast with doodles. That night, she counted the number of hearts drawn on her cast and briefly felt good about herself. This version of herself was one she had a hard time reconciling with. Even as she looked in the mirror, she didn't recognize herself. *How could you?* she wanted to ask herself, not Jong-su.

"What's that number?" Jae-yon pointed at a phone number on Tae-hee's cast.

"Some guy?"

"So soon? Didn't you just break up?"

"Break up with who?"

"You were going out with Jong-su again, no?"

"Why would you think that?"

"Tae-hee, we've known each other for over thirteen years," Jae-yon rolled her eyes. "Pretending to be fooled, watching you try to lie—it gets old."

기가 등장한다. 이것이 정말 미래의 시작을 알리는 현재의 끝인 걸까. 그런 장면들은 낱낱이 거짓말이다. 그건 비 내리는 날, 3년간 사귄 연인과 악수하며 헤어지는 연인을 보며 그들의 사랑이 끝났다고 믿는 것과 비슷하다. 세상에 후회보다 먼저 도착하는 깨달음은 없다.

실수로 그의 사진에 '좋아요'를 누를 수 있겠지만, 잠시 민망하면 그뿐이다. 하지만 헤어진 사람이 옛 연인을 다시 만난다는 건 전혀 다른 문제였다. 끝난 줄 알았던 사랑이 다시 시작됐다면 그건 사랑이 아닌 다른 감정이 개입했을 가능성이 크다. 그것이 시기심인지 모멸감인지 집착인지는 중요하지 않다. 다만 그것이 무엇이든 도저히 멈출 방법이 떠오르지 않는다는 것이다. 그런데 하느님이 보우하사 그날

왼쪽 다리와 오른손 검지가 동시에 부러진 것이다.

아무것도 할 수 없었다. 태희는 적어도 7주 동안 회사 워크숍에도, 재테크 소모임에도, 일본어 학원에도, 수영장에도 갈 수 없었다. 꼼짝없이 인터넷으로 주문한 브로콜리 스프를 마시며 침대에 누워 있어야 했다. 침대

Tae-hee knew. The fact that your ex dumped you to get back together with the girl he dumped for you, was not a good reason to get back together with him. It's not that she didn't know how irrational and emotional a decision it was. Everyone knows that you'll probably break something if you jump out of a moving cab. But what about this: not everyone can predict that the cab that's been parked on Hannam Motorway in a deadlock would move at the very moment you jump out of the cab. There. Not that the excuse can unbreak your leg.

So many movies out there end with an airport scene. The final scene signaling a new beginning features the image of a plane taking off. Is that really the end of the present and the beginning of the future? These scenes are 100 percent fiction. It's as naïve as watching a three-year relationship end with a civilized handshake on a rainy day and actually believing that their relationship is over. No epiphany on earth travels faster than regret.

Your finger can slip and accidentally hit "Like" on his profile picture. You'll be embarrassed, but it'll pass soon enough. But getting back together with your ex is a completely different matter. If a love that's ended comes back to life, there's a good

에만 누워 있자니, 병문안을 알리는 친구들의 문자가 속속 들어왔다. "김태희! 너 택시에서 뛰어내렸다며? 미친! 내가 크레이지 버거 열 개 사 갈 테니 배 터지게 그거나 먹어!" 광기가 꼭 나쁘기만 한 게 아니다. 광기는 끝을 불러오기 때문이다. 파국이란 말 뒤에 남는 건 폐허고, 폐사지 같아진 마음속에서 부는 바람은 더 이상 뜨겁지 않았다. 그런 것들을 알아가게 된 시간이었다.

태희는 자신의 스마트폰 가만히 바라봤다.

깨진 액정은 고치지 않을 생각이었다.

8.

태희가 이종수와 헤어진 건 3주일 전이었다.

태희에겐 다섯 번째 이별이었다.

9.

종수와 다시 만나기 전, 짧은 연애가 있었다.

깁스에 자신의 번호를 기록했던 남자는 종수의 대학 동아리 선배였다. 자신의 인생이야 어찌 되든 상대의 마음을 아프게 할 수만 있다면 못 할 게 없는 상태. 그것이 '미저리의 마음'이었다. 전 남자친구 증후군과 미저

chance it was reignited by something other than love. It doesn't matter if it was jealousy, humiliation, or obsession. What matters is that you can't think of a way to hit the breaks. But that day, by divine intervention, Tae-hee broke her left leg and her right thumb at the same time.

She was completely out of commission. For seven weeks, Tae-hee couldn't attend company workshops, investment club meetings, Japanese classes, or swim lessons. She had to lie in bed and eat broccoli soup she ordered off the Internet. Friends sent good wishes via text. *Tae-hee Kim! I heard you jump out of a moving cab. You crazy! Feast on these ten crazy burger emojis. Get well soon!* Madness isn't always bad. Madness drives the plot to the finale. Obliteration leaves the scene in ruins, and the gusts of wind that blows through your demolished temple of a heart is feverish no more. Live and learn.

Tae-hee looked down at her phone.

She had no plans to replace the cracked screen.

8.

Three weeks had gone by since Tae-hee and Jong-su broke up.

리의 마음이란 조어를 스스로에게 처방 약처럼 제조하던 시간, 태희는 미루고 미루던 핸드메이드 의자 업체의 대표와 미팅을 진행했다.

"100년을 쓸 수 있는 의자라는 게 사람들의 마음을 사로잡는단 생각은 들지 않습니다. 사람들은 오래 쓸 수 있는 물건을 더 이상 원하지 않으니까요."

"오래 쓸 수 있는 제품을 싫어한다고요?"

대표가 의아한 얼굴로 태희를 바라봤다.

"네. 고장이 나야 죄책감을 가지지 않고 쉽게 물건을 버릴 수 있으니까요. 저라면 고쳐서라도 쓰고 싶은 사람을 만나고 싶을 것 같습니다."

대표가 태희를 빤히 바라봤다.

"김 프로님, 방금 물건을 사람으로 잘못 말한 거 아십니까?"

"네?"

태희는 대표를 멍하게 바라봤다.

실수였다.

그것이 자문자답이든, 오답이든, 그 무엇이든 웃음이 터져 나왔다.

"김태희 씨, 이름만큼 재밌는 분이시네."

This was Tae-hee's fifth breakup.

9.

Tae-hee had a brief fling before getting back together with Jong-su.

The guy who left the phone number on her cast was a guy a few years ahead in Jong-su's college club. Tae-hee met him in her "misery state", a condition in which one is willing to do anything to hurt an ex, even at one's own expense. During this phase when she was self-diagnosing with made-up terms like "ex-boyfriend syndrome" and "misery state" to justify her actions, Tae-hee finally had the meeting with the custom-made chair company rep she'd been putting off forever.

"I don't think the concept of a chair that lasts a hundred years will entice customers. People no longer want products that last."

"People don't want products that last?" The rep gave her a funny look.

"That's right," she said. "in order to throw a product away guilt-free, the product has to break. I, on the other hand, would like someone I like enough to go to the trouble of fixing up."

The rep stared squarely at Tae-hee and said,

대표는 웃고 있는 태희를 오랫동안 바라봤다.

이성에게 잘 보이고 싶다는 마음이 없을 때, 역설적으로 자신이 가진 매력은 증폭된다. 광고는 제품을 다루는 일처럼 보이지만 결국 사람의 욕망을 읽는 일이다. 그 잠깐의 연애 동안, 태희는 뜻밖에 자신에 대해 몰랐던 또 다른 자신의 성격을 발견했다.

연애는 나인 줄 알았던 내가 변해가는 과정을 지켜보는 일이다. 그 변화가 마음에 든다면, 참을 만하다면, 그 연애는 얼마간 이어진다. 그러다가 '나인 줄 알았던 나'와 '그가 보는 나 사이'의 갈등이 더 이상 좁혀지지 않을 때 끝나는 것이다.

이때, 이별이 남긴 새로운 성격은 유품처럼 남는다. 연애는 망해도 시간은 빠르게 가고, 있는 힘껏 나이도 먹는다. 다만 질문은 남는다.

"종수야. 나 너랑 제대로 헤어지고 싶어서 다시 만난 거야."

미저리의 마음이 연애의 끝이라면, 그것이 꼭 새드 엔딩인 걸까. 하지 말았어야 할 말과 꼭 했어야 하는 말 중 무엇이 더 사람의 마음을 끝까지 아프게 하는 걸까. 사랑은 죽어도, 종수가 선물한 화분은 아직 죽지 않았다.

"You meant to say 'chair,' right? You said 'some-one.'"

"Excuse me?" Tae-hee stared back with a dumb look on her face.

That turned out to be a mistake. Laughter—Was it an answer to her own question, a wrong answer, or a whatever?—burst out of her.

"Tae-hee Kim, you're a funny, funny lady." the rep gave her a good, long stare and she continued to cackle.

When you stop trying to be attractive, you ironically become much more charming. Marketing appears to be a business of dealing with products, but it's ultimately about understanding human desire. During that brief relationship, Tae-hee discovered a side of herself she didn't know she had.

Dating is a process of observing the transformation of what you were sure was your "self." If you like what you're becoming, or if it's tolerable at least, the relationship goes on for a while. Then when you reach the point where the gap between "what you were sure was your 'self'" and "how he sees you" cannot be closed anymore, the relationship is over.

The relationship is over, but you get to keep the

키우고 있는 상추는 뽑아도 뽑아도 자력갱생하듯 다시 자랐다.

옆집 고양이가 창문 위에 앉아 있었다.

왼쪽 엉덩이를 내민 채 앉아 있는 삐딱함이 태희는 무척 마음에 들었다. 고양이는 신기하기도 해서, 살아 움직이는 액자처럼 자신이 앉아 있는 모든 곳을 근사한 그림으로 만든다. 그림 같은 풍경이었을 것이다. 고양이와 웃고 있는 종수를 찍던 순간, 그의 옛 연인도 틀림없이 자신처럼 그렇게 생각했을 것이다.

날씨 보듯 확인하는 미세먼지 앱에는 '현재 상태 최고'라는 말이 적혀 있었다. 1이라고 적힌 미세 먼지 수치가 반짝거렸다. 간만에 보는 쾌적한 수치였다. 태희에게 1이 숫자로 읽히지 않은 지 오래였다. 그것은 아직 그녀에게 읽지 않은 메시지를 뜻하는 1이었고, 구체적으로 종수가 전달하고자 하는 침묵의 한 형태였다.

그 침묵이 너무 시끄러워 문득 귀를 막고 싶었다.

창문을 활짝 열었다.

3일 만이었다.

newly discovered "self" like a memento. Relationships crash and burn, but time marches on, and
you age to the sedulous beat of its drum. Still, one
question remains.

"Jong-su, I got back together with you so I could
have a proper do-over of our breakup."

If the relationship ends in "misery state", is that
necessarily a tragic ending? Which ache is more intense and enduring—what you really shouldn't have
said, or what you really should have said?

Love was dead, but the potted plant that Jong-su
gave her was still alive. She could rip out the let-
tuce until kingdom come, and yet still more sprung
up like a phoenix from the ashes.

The neighbor's cat was perched on the window-
sill. Tae-hee very much enjoyed the insouciance of
the cat in a half-sphinx position, left bum casually
sticking out. Cats have a way of making any scene
picturesque. *What a pretty picture*, she must have
thought, just as Tae-hee had, when she captured
the moment Jong-su was smiling with the cat.

The Air Quality Index app she checked like the
weather read "Current Index: Excellent." The aqi
number was a shining "1," a number she hadn't
seen on the app in a long time. "1" turned from Ar-

abic numeral to "unread message" a long time ago, more specifically a form of insistent silence coming from Jong-su via KakaoTalk.

The silence was so raucous she wanted to cover her ears.

She opened the windows all the way.
For the first time in three days.

창작노트
Writer's Note

우리 시대의 이별에 대한 얘길 해보고 싶었다. 과거, 사람을 찾는 프로그램이 있을 정도로 이별은 단절을 의미했다. 입학이 있으면 졸업이 있었던 셈. 하지만 지금 과거의 사람들이라는 말은 시대착오적이다. 24시간 연결된 SNS 세상에서 우리는 이제 친구, 친구의 친구, 아는 사람, 알 수도 있는 사람으로 연결되어 있다. 이별은 의지의 문제가 아니라 이제 구조의 문제가 되어가고 있다.

현대의 이별은 정확히 말해 이별의 이별이다. 이별은 한 번의 이별로 끝나지 않고, 여러 번의 과정을 걸쳐 끝내 완성된다. 우리는 이제 어떤 식으로든 연결되어 있

I wanted to write about breakups of our time. In the past, breaking up meant complete severing of ties—so much so that there were TV shows devoted to helping people find their past lovers, out of touch for years. Beginning a relationship naturally entailed the end of it. But nowadays, the phrase "past lover" sounds somewhat anachronistic. In the world of social media, we are connected 24 hours with our friends, friends' friends, people we know, and people we may know. These days, breaking up is not about our willpower, but about social institutions.

Breakup after the breakup—this is what breaking

다. 차단, 삭제, 끊기를 통해 인연을 끊으려 해도 어떤 식으로든 연결되어 이별이 내 현재를 재구성하기도 한다. 상대의 일상을 스토킹 할 수 있는 SNS 환경 때문에 우연을 빙자해 만남은 지속된다. 만남의 문턱은 낮아졌지만 이별의 문턱은 자꾸만 높아지고 있다. 하지만 오히려 입문식은 다양해지고, 출문식은 여전히 빈곤하다. 헤어지고 싶어도 헤어지지 못하는 사람들, 헤어지는 중인 사람들이 계속 증가하고 있는 것이다.

이제 전남자친구나 전여자친구라는 말은 종결된 과거의 사람이 아니라, 현재의 나를 재구성하는 또 다른 종족처럼 느껴진다. 영화나 드라마 수많은 문학 작품에서 과거의 사람들이 자주 등장하는 건, 더 이상 그들이 과거의 유령이 아니라 현재에 출몰하는 '현시'이기 때문이다.

이런 혼란스러움 속에서 사람들은 최대한 안전한 사랑을 찾기 위해 노력한다. 안전이 의미하는 바는 점점 '안정'이 되어간다. 안전하면서 동시에 자유로운 삶을 꿈꾸는 사람들에게 연애는 점점 더 불안해지기만 한다.

up actually means these days. A relationship doesn'
t end with a single breakup, but needs further
breakups to finally come to an end. Every one of
us is connected in every possible way. We try to
sever our ties by blocking, deleting, or unfollowing,
yet we still find ourselves somehow so tenaciously
connected that our past breakups often reconstruct
our present. Social media, which allows us to stalk
our exes, perpetuates our relationship and engi-
neer "coincidences." While today's dating has lower
entry barriers than before, the threshold of breakup has become higher than ever. We have so many
ways to enter into a relationship, but few ways to
get out. As a result, more and more couples who
want to break up are stuck in their relationship, or
forever "in the process of" breaking up.

These days, the term ex-boyfriend or ex-girlfriend means no longer a person of the closed
past, but rather feels like another species that re-
constructs who we are in the present. Many films
or literary works feature people of the past, not
because they are ghosts from the past but because
they are manifestations haunting the present.

Amid this confusion, people strive to seek the

SNS에는 잠재적 연애 대상자들이 널려 있다. 빨리 선택하면 손해라는 현대의 계산법이 점점 더 많은 사람들을 헤매게 만든다. 하지만 선택지가 늘어날수록 우리는 점점 더 불안해진다. 인터넷에는 처음과 끝이 없다. 어떤 것을 선택해도 그것보다 더 좋은 것이 있을 것이라는 '가성비의 악몽'이 늘 잠재해 있는 것이다. 결정 장애는 현대병이다. 108개의 선택지 대신 5개의 선택지에서 고른 아이스크림을 훨씬 더 선호한다는 건 이른바 선택의 역설을 얘기한다.

잠재적 연애 대상자가 있는 한 연애의 불안은 계속될 것이다. 연애불능자는 곧 사랑불능자로 그들은 진짜 사랑을 위해선 '선택과 가능성의 문을 닫아야 한다는 것'을 모른다.

현대의 사랑이란 이제 자기 정체성을 찾기 위한 하나의 과정에 가까워지고 있다. 스마트폰의 표피처럼 기스 없는 완벽함에 갈망이 사랑에까지 개입해 자아계발의 한 측면에서 사랑을 생각하는 사람들이 많아지기 시작한 것이다. 연애불능은 그렇게 심화된다.

safest love possible. "Safety" has become closer in connotation to "stability." Those who wish their life to be both safe and free feel more anxious about dating. Social media is flooded with potential dating partners, but people on the dating market can't shake off the modern maxim "the sooner you choose, the more you lose." The Internet has no beginning or end. The nightmare of cost-effectiveness lurks there: whatever you choose, there will be always better choices. Indecisiveness is a modern disorder. The study that shows people much more prefer ice cream flavors they chose out of five options, rather than 108, indicates the so-called "paradox of choice."

As long as there are potential dating partners, the anxiety of dating will continue. Dating incompetence equals inability to love. The sufferers do not know that they should close the door of choices and possibilities to find their real love.

Modern love has come to resemble a process of self-discovery. More people have come to think of love as a path of self-development, out of the desire for the perfectly blemish-free finishes like the smooth screen of a smartphone. As a result, dating

있는 그대로의 나를 인정받고 싶다는 갈망은 상대를 결함 많은 존재로 새롭게 규정한다. 있는 그대로의 나를 사랑해달라면서, 있는 그대로의 상대는 인정하지 못하는 것이다. 여기엔 오류가 있다. 상대가 바뀐다면 나는 좋은 연애를 할 것이다. 지금까지의 연애에 실패한 이유는 내가 잘못된 상대를 골랐기 때문이라고 생각하는 것이다. 결국 대개의 문제는 '내' 문제이기 때문에 이것은 치밀한 자기 기만의 결과다.

강남의 사교육 현장에서 명문대를 나온 주인공은 모든 것들을 '공부'하는 것으로 삶의 난관을 돌파해왔다. 감정보다 학습이 먼저였고, 이해보다 분석이 먼저였다. 점수를 올려 명문대에 진학하려는 목표지향적 성격이 가져온 후천적 결과물이었다.

광고회사의 카피라이터로 일하는 주인공은 현대인의 욕망을 뒤좇으며 우리 시대의 사랑을 물건의 구매 행위에 빗댄다. 고장 난 것을 고쳐 쓰지 않고, 새로운 것을 싼값에 쉽게 사들이는 현대의 쇼핑법과 사랑이 크게 다르지 않다는 것이다. 이별마저도 자기계발의 소재로 삼

incompetence worsens. The desire to be accepted as we are defines others as faulty and flawed. In other words, we ask others to love us as we are, but never accept others as they are. Therein lies a fallacy: *If I chose another person, I would have a better relationship. The reason I have failed in relationship so far is that I went for the wrong one.* But this idea is nothing but self-deception, since most of the problems are all about "me, myself, and I."

Tae-hee, who went through the "Gang-nam private education mill" and entered a prestigious college, has always found breakthroughs in her struggles by studying. Learning came before feeling, and analyzing before understanding. This was the product of her goal-oriented personality that had contributed to her getting higher scores and entering a prestigious college.

As a copywriter, Tae-hee seeks after the desire of modern people and draws an analogy of modern love from product consumption. People don't mend things, but replace them with new, cheap ones, which isn't much different from how we love these days. Tae-hee's struggles to turn a breakup into an opportunity for self-improvement leave us

아 승화시키려는 주인공의 안간힘을 보면서 현대적 의미에서의 '실용성' 혹은 '효율성'에 대해서도 되짚어 보고 싶었다. 감정은 정량화될 수 있을까. 액체가 끓어 기체가 되는 것처럼 자신의 비참과 절망마저도 성장의 동력으로 승화시키려는 이런 노력이 효용과 효율에 대한 신경증에 시달리는 우리 시대의 청춘의 내면에 어떤 영향을 끼치는지에 대해서 묻고 싶다. 과거의 이별과 지금의 이별이 어떻게 다른 차원에 진입했는지도 말이다.

wondering about so-called "practicality" and "efficiency" in the modern sense. Can we quantify our emotions? Like liquid boils and turns to gas, Taehee strives to sublimate her misery and desperation into a driving force for internal growth. I want to ask you how this struggle has influenced the mentality of the young generation these days who suffer from neurotic desire for utility and efficiency. And compared to the past, how breaking up of our time has entered a different dimension.

해설
Commentary

읽기의 사랑, 사랑의 읽기

안서현 (문학평론가)

　제목만 살펴보아도 알 수 있다.『아주 보통의 연애』
『애인의 애인에게』『실연당한 사람들의 일곱 시 조찬 모
임』. 백영옥이 사랑과 이별의 작가, 연애의 풍속을 그리
는 작가, '연애소설 장인'이라는 것을 말이다.

　백영옥의 단편소설「연애의 감정학」역시 사랑의 새
로운 풍속도를 그려내고 있는 작품이다. 그 신 풍속이
란 바로 '읽기의 사랑'이다. 우리는 끊임없이 읽는다. 모
두가 휴대전화를 비롯한 모바일 기기로 끊임없이 웹에
접속하는 시대, 손안의 단말기가 마치 우리 몸의 일부
인 것처럼 연장된 신체로 기능하는 시대다. 몸의 감각
이 변화하니, 연애의 풍경 역시 바뀔 수밖에 없다.

How We Love Like a Reader: On Reading Love

Ahn Seo-hyeon (literary critic)

Perfectly Normal Romance, To My Lover's Lover, and *7AM Breakfast Gathering of the Dumped*—these book titles tell one that Baek Young-ok is an author with a keen interest in the romance, love and its aftermath, and the conventions of modern love.

Baek's short story *How to Break Up Like a Winner* portrays the newest practices of love: which are also the love of a reader. People read relentlessly these days; they are constantly accessing the internet with various mobile devices, including smartphones, which now function as part of their physical selves. Thus, the landscape of our romantic lives is bound to evolve along with what might be

주인공 태희는 이별 후 자신의 '패배'의 원인을 찾기 위해 부지런히 책을 찾아 읽고 동영상도 섭렵한다. 자신의 이별을 심리학과 각종 연애 지침들을 바탕으로 분석한다. 애착 유형에 대한 이론은 태희와 그녀의 연인이었던 종수가 처음 사랑에 빠진 까닭부터 헤어지게 된 이유까지를 설명해주는 듯하다. 또 이별 후 다시 만나 행복해진 연인들에 대한 통계는 이들의 미래에 대한 해답을 제시해줄 수 있을 것만 같다. 이러한 것들이 사랑에 대한 '객관적' 데이터라고 태희는 믿는다. 연애의 감정에 대한 과학적 접근이 가능하다면 바로 이러한 이론이나 통계를 통해서일 것이다. 가장 비합리적인 인간의 행동인 사랑, 그것에 대해 합리적으로 설명하고자 하는 역설의 과학이다.

점차 태희는 사랑에 관한 일반적으로 참조 가능한 데이터만이 아니라 상대 종수에 대한 데이터 읽기의 단계로 이행한다. 이별 직후 비활성화했던 소셜 네트워크 서비스 계정을 복구한 것이다. 그에 대한 일종의 '데이터 마이닝', 다시 말해 SNS에 올라온 그의 일상의 흔적들을 추적하는 일에 골몰하게 된다. 연애를 할 당시에조차 알지 못했던 연인의 과거까지도 알게 된다.

called our "changing bodies."

After breaking up with Jong-su, Tae-hee tries to find the reason why she was "defeated," by reading books and watching video clips. She analyzes her breakup based on psychology and self-help books on relationships. The theories on attachment types seem to explain the whole story, from why they fell for each other in the first place, all the way to why they broke up. The statistics on couples that break up and get back together seem to give her a glimpse of their future relationship. These are "objective" data on love, she believes. If any scientific approach could draw a critical appraisal of dating, it would be through these theories and statistics. She strives to present a rational explanation for the most irrational of human behaviors—love, A true paradox of science.

Tae-hee's analytical focal point gradually shifts, though, from general data on dating to specific data about her ex-boyfriend Jong-su. She reactivates her social media account, which she had deactivated right after the break up. And she becomes absorbed in "data-mining," that is, tracking the traces of his life revealed through the feeds of various social networking sites. In the process, she

이러한 데이터는 처음에는 보고 싶지 않아도 태희의 눈에 들어와서 보게 되고, 보다 보면 상대에 대해 더 많은 것들이 보여서 또 보게 되고, 그러다 보면 또 다른 숨겨진 상대의 면모를 알고 싶다는 욕망이 생겨 또 보게 된다. 그래서 점점 더 그의 데이터들을 깊숙이 파고들게 된다. 그래서 작가는 '초연결 사회'라는 말을 꺼낸다. 원하지 않더라도 서로 촘촘하게 연결되어 있는 사회다. 그리고 서로 연결된 이들에 대한, 오래되었거나 새로 생성된 데이터들에 쉽게 접근 가능하다. '초연결 사회'일 뿐 아니라 '완전기록 사회'이기에 가능한 일이다. 원하지 않더라도 어느새 빼곡하게 기록이 남는다. 기록의 운명으로부터 도망치기는 쉽지 않다. 그것들은 사라지지는 않고 쌓이기만 한다. 태희는 카피라이터답게, 상대가 남에게 보여주고 싶지 않아 하는 것들을 추적한다. 상대방의 과거, 그중의 찢어진 페이지다.

태희는 종수의 남모르는 과거에 대해 하나둘 알아갈수록 자신이 '이 상황을 통제하고 있다'는 착각을 하게 된다. 그러나 실상은 반대다. 상대방의 과거와 헤어지고 난 뒤 현재의 모습을 속속들이 알게 되자, 복잡하게 얽힌 감정의 정리는 더욱 쉽지 않게 된다. 이쯤 되면 궁

learns new things about his past.

Data on her ex-boyfriend—whether she wants to see them or not—catch her eye, and once she notices them, say something about him that further provoke her desire to peer into his hidden life and tempt her to keep digging. At this point, the term "hyper-connectivity" comes up and the fact that in this "hyper-connected" society, we are closely joined to one another, regardless of our wishes for it. We can easily access old or newly generated data about those people interconnected with us, because we are living in a society of not only hyper-connectivity but also permanent records. Once we upload something onto the web, it never disappears. We are doomed to be "saved"—a reality from which no one can be saved. Records never disappear, but only accumulate. Tae-hee, who works as a copywriter, goes after what her ex-boyfriend doesn't want others to see: his past and, specifically, pages he "tore out."

As Tae-hee finds out about Jong-su's hidden past, layer by layer, she feels in control of the situation. Yet just the reverse is true. Knowing more about her ex's past and present instead makes it difficult for her to sort out her feelings. Data per-

금해진다. 데이터가 끊임없이 사랑을 부추긴다. 그렇다면, 우리는 연인을 잊지 못하는 것인가, 단지 연인의 데이터로부터 벗어나지 못하는 것인가?

모든 정보를 끊임없이 업그레이드하지 않으면 불안한, 그리고 원하지 않는 데이터까지도 '데이터 스모그'의 형태로 계속 접하지 않으면 안 되는 과잉 정보화 시대다. 우리가 하고 있는 것은 '데이터의 사랑'이 아닐까? 끊임없이 데이터를 수집하고, 그것을 읽고, 그것에 기반하여 서사를 만들어내고, 그것을 해석하고, 또 그것을 재해석한다. 주인공인 태희가 광고 일에 종사한다는 것은 의미심장하다. 광고는 상품 판매량이나 소비자 행동에 관한 데이터를 가장 많이 다루고 참조하는 일이자 소비자 대중에게 그들이 원치 않더라도 끊임없이 상품에 대한 데이터를 은근슬쩍 제공하는 일이기 때문이다. 미세먼지에 대한 이야기가 계속되는 것 역시 하나의 상징일 것이다. 그것은 우리의 시야를 흐려놓고, 또 비가 내려도 도무지 가시지 않으면서 우리로 하여금 그것으로부터 벗어날 수 없다는 느낌을 갖게 하는 것이다. 눈앞을 제대로 보지 못하고 있다는 느낌도 든다. 보고 싶다는 욕망은 점점 더해가서, 택시에서 뛰어내릴 만큼

petuate love. At this point, we are curious: What is it that one truly can't get over: the ex—or the data of ex?

In the age of "information surplus," we feel anxious unless we are constantly updating all the information we have, as well as inhaling unwanted information from the "data smog." Indeed, perhaps our modern love is "data love." We relentlessly collect and analyze data, create narratives based on the analyses, interpret them, and then re-interpret our interpretations. Tae-hee's choice of a livelihood, marketing, is telling because it is all about data, on product sales or consumer behaviors, and exposing consumers to information about products —whether they are aware of it or not. Particulate matter, referred to throughout the story, is also a symbol. It obscures our sight, remains suspended in the air even after a heavy rain, and gives us the impression that we can never escape from it. It also inhibits our ability to see what's in front of us. The desire to see things clearly builds up to the point in this story that a grown woman jumps out of a moving taxi.

Tae-hee—"homo ex data" incarnate—sees Jong-su again. In the process of getting back together,

커지는 것이다.

우리의 데이터적 인간, 태희는 결국 다시 종수를 만난다. 종수를 다시 만나는 과정에서 연이어 네 번째, 그리고 다섯 번째의 연애를 한다. 태희의 종수에 대한 변하지 않은 사랑의 마음 때문일까? 종수는 태희에게 고쳐서라도 다시 만나고 싶은 '불멸의 걸작', 아니 불멸의 연인인 것일까. 그런데 그녀는 오히려 종수와 "제대로 헤어지기 위해", 즉 고쳐서라도 다시 헤어지기 위해 그를 만난 것이다. 그것은 말하자면 종수와의 연애에 대한 데이터의 마지막 정리와도 같은 것이다. 자신의 세 번째 사랑에 대한 데이터를 다시 읽고 잘못된 부분을 덧쓰기 위한 것, 말하자면 사랑의 오류를 고치고 재정리하기 위한 것이다. 그리하여 다음 사랑에 관한 새로운 데이터를 생성해나갈 수 있는 준비를 하는 것이다. 그것은 '데이터의 사랑'의 끝과 그것으로부터의 해방처럼 보이기도 하지만, 결국은 그 과정 역시 다섯 번째 사랑과 이별이라는 짧은 기록으로 환원된다. '데이터의 사랑'은 앞으로도 계속되는 것이다.

이렇게 보면 이 소설은 '읽기의 사랑', 즉 '데이터의 사랑'이라는 애정의 풍속을 그리고 있다고 할 수 있겠다.

she goes through her fourth, and then fifth romantic relationships. Is it because Tae-hee's feelings for Jong-su had never changed? Then is Jong-su an "immortal masterpiece," or the "immortal lover" she wants to "go to the trouble of fixing up?" She claims that she got back together with Jong-su to "have a proper do-over" of their breakup. And this phase requires a final one of data processing on her relationship with him, including re-reading the data on her third love and re-writing the wrong parts. In other words, she has to fix any errors and put things in order, preparing to generate new data on the next love. This final stage looks like a grand termination of and liberation from "data love." Yet it is reduced to another short data list, titled "fifth love and breakup." Once again, "data love" persists.

This story is indeed about the codes of "data love," or "love like a reader." But there is another layer in this story about more fundamental aspects of love and breakup. What does love or breakup mean for the subject? This question leads us to another topic: how we read love.

Throughout the story, Tae-hee reads and interprets every breakup she experiences. The reasons are analyzed in several ways: Her lover has an

그런데 이 소설은 다른 방식으로 한 번 더 읽을 수 있다. 더 본질적인 사랑과 이별의 이야기를 들려주는 것으로도 읽을 수 있는 것이다. 사랑과 이별은 우리에게 무엇인가? 이 질문을 따라가며 소설을 읽다 보면, 우리는 이번에는 '사랑의 읽기'라는 화두를 만나게 된다.

태희는 자신이 마주하게 된 이별의 사건을 읽고 있다. 즉 해석하는 것이다. 그 사건은 여러 가지로 해석된다. 종수가 회피성 애착이어서, 태희가 불안성 애착이라서, 종수를 믿을 수 없어서, 종수가 양다리를 걸쳐서, 종수가 먼저 헤어지자고 해서……. 이 사건에 대한 읽기만으로도 쉽게 끝날 것 같지 않다.

그런데 이러한 해석만으로는 충분하지 않다. 태희는 상대에 대한 더 심도 있는 읽기의 작업을 계속하게 된다. 다시 말해 '전 남자친구 증후군'이라는 해석의 병에 걸리게 되는 것이다. 그녀는 '찢겨진 책'과도 같은 종수라는 사람을 다시 해석해나간다. 그의 숨겨진 과거, 그가 자신에 대해 지우고 싶어 했던 것들, 그가 만나고 있는 것이 예전 헤어진 여자친구라는 사실…… 그런 모든 사실들을 샅샅이 읽고, 또 태희는 종수라는 책을 뒤늦게 이해할 수 있게 된다. 우리는 늘 사랑이 끝나고 난

avoidant attachment style; she is an anxious attachment type; she couldn't trust him; he cheated on
her; he was the one who said "Let's break up." The
list goes on.

Yet all those interpretations are not enough. Tae-
hee continues her reading of her ex-lover, this
time in more depth. Her act of reading becomes
more like an obsession, the so-called "ex-boyfriend syndrome." She re-analyzes her ex-boyfriend, who seems like a book with pages torn out.
The missing pages turn out to contain his hidden
past, parts he wanted to delete, and also the fact
that he is dating his ex-girlfriend again. Only after
scrupulously reading the content does she truly
understand the entire book, which might be titled
Jong-su Lee. Likewise, we modern creatures understand our beloved, but always belatedly, only after
the love ends.

The remaining aspect for Tae-hee is reading
herself. In fact, the relationship will never be fin-
ished until she thoroughly explores the complexity
of her own love. This is the reason why she goes
through the fifth relationship and breakup. She
needs one more round to "read" her inner self.
That fifth love entails the yearning for a person she

후에 상대를 비로소 이해할 수 있게 되는 것이다.

　이제 태희는 마지막으로 자신을 읽어야 한다. 자신 안에 있는 사랑의 복잡성을 다 읽어낼 때까지 이번 연애는 끝나지 않을 것이다. 그녀가 다시 다섯 번째 사랑과 이별을 하게 되는 이유 역시 같은 것이다. 자기 자신을 다 읽어내기 위하여 그녀는 이 한 번의 기회를 더 필요로 했던 것이다. 그 다섯 번째 사랑은 고쳐서라도 만나고 싶은 상대를 찾고 싶다는 마음이었고, 모든 것이 그림 같이 보이는 사랑의 환상에서 벗어나고 싶다는 마음이었고, 상대를 아프게 하고 싶은 '미저리의 마음'이었고, 진심이 아닌 진실을 대면하고 싶다는 마음이었으며, 사랑이 아닌 배신감과 모멸감과 집착과 같은 다른 감정들이 얽힌 덩어리의 마음이었고, 잃는 것을 더 힘들어하는 마음이었으며, 또 무엇보다도 제대로 헤어지고 싶다는 마음이었다. 이러한 자신의 마음들을 읽어내고 나자 태희는 후련해진다. 더 이상 세상 밖과 마음속의 계절이 다르지 않다. 그것은 꼭 종수에게 복수를 했기 때문은 아니다. 두 사람의 사랑과 이별에 대해서는 물론, 상대에 대해, 그리고 자신에 대해 모든 해석이 끝난 것이다. '감정학'의 한 단계가 끝을 고한 것이다. 그것

would love enough to go to the trouble of improv-
ing; the urge to escape from a picturesque fantasy
of love; the "misery state" of wanting to hurt her
ex; the determination to face the facts, not her
faith; mixed feelings of betrayal, contempt, and
obsession; her vulnerability to loss; and, most of
all, her desire to have a proper and thorough ending. After reading through her layers of feelings and
emotions, she finally feels free. Her internal climate
is no longer distant from external reality. This is not
just because she gets revenge, but because she is
able to go through all the processes of interpreting
Jong-su, her relationship with him, and herself.
This puts an end to the process of her appraisal,
leaving her with a deeper understanding of the nature of love and of being human.

For Tae-hee, and every other contemporary lover, falling in love and breaking up encompass the
act of reading. The beginning and the end of a relationship give us an opportunity to open the "cover" of ourselves and ones we love and loved. In
this sense, all romantic love is a form of reading.
Only after we finish reading all the materials within
the relationship can we start a new chapter in our
own lives. Or like the sky after clouds of fine dust

은 사랑의 본질, 그리고 나아가 인간에 대해 한 단계 더 이해하는 과정이었다고도 할 수 있다.

태희의 사랑은 물론 모든 사랑과 이별은 읽기의 행위와도 닮아 있는지 모른다. 사랑과 이별은 자신과 상대에 대한 책을 펼쳐볼 수 있는 기회라고도 할 수 있을 것이다. 결국 연애는 인생의 독서와도 같다는 비유가 가능해진다. 미세먼지가 없는 맑은 날과도 같이 모든 것을 다 읽고 났을 때, 비로소 우리는 인생의 한 장을 또 넘길 수 있다. 백영옥 작가가 그려내는 '읽기의 사랑'과 '사랑의 읽기', 거기에는 이 시대 사랑의 풍속은 물론, 우리에게 삶을 가르치는 사랑의 영원한 본질도 포착되어 있는 것이다.

안서현 2010년 월간 《문학사상》 신인상(평론 부문)을 수상하며 작품활동을 시작했다. 계간 《학산문학》 편집위원을 지내고 있다.

particles have cleared up. Baek's portrayal of how we love like a reader, and how we read our love, captures not only the latest trends in dating but also the lasting effect of love as a life lesson.

An Seo-hyeon An Seo-hyeon made her literary debut in 2010, when she won the monthly *Munhaksasang* New Writer Award in the category of literary criticism. She currently serves on the editorial board of the quarterly *Haksanmunhak*.

비평의 목소리
Critical Acclaim

백영옥은 백영옥 스타일로 독자들에게 계속 남아 있을 것 같다. 약간은 빤하지만 모든 것이 공개되는 사회가 갈수록 더 '인간은 그만큼 관계를 통해 자신의 정체성을 확인하는 고도로 사회화된 존재'(『빨간 머리 앤이 하는 말』中에서)가 될 것이 확실하기 때문이다. 그런 시대에 인간은 오히려 어느 곳에나 존재하지만 어느 곳에도 존재하지 않는 몰개성화된 존재가 될 것도 빤하다. 그런 점에서 백영옥이 소설 산문으로 읽어주는 우리 시대의 모습은 신선하게 느껴질 것 같다는 기대감이 들게 한다.

조창완, 「참을 수 없는 시대의 가벼움을 버리다,
백영옥이 주목되는 까닭」, 시사저널, 2017

Baek is known for her distinctive "Baek Young-ok style." In a society where everything is open to everyone—obvious as it sounds—we humans become "highly social animals who affirm their identities in relationship with others." (from *Words of Anne of Green Gables*) Also obvious is that humans will be more and more de-individualized, to the extent of being everybody and nobody. Ironically, in this sense, we can expect Baek's characteristic portrayal of our times in her next novels and essays to be as telling as ever.

Cho Chang-wan, The Unbearable(and Forgeable) Lightness of Being-Why We Read Baek Young-ok, *Sisajournal*, 2017

우리는 왜 '무엇'을 매개로 소통하고, '무엇' 뒤에 숨어 자신을 보호하고, '무엇'의 역할로 자신을 축소시킬까. 체험의 직접성이 사라져가는 시대 속에서 사람들은 점점 더 기계화된 역할 속에 스스로를 가두고, 자신의 이미지를 포장하는 각종 '디지털 아바타'를 만들어 자신의 육체를 대신하려 한다. 스스로를 자신의 그림자로, 부차적 분신으로 만드는 '원본-주체'의 고통이야말로 백영옥의 단편들이 일관되게 보여주는 테마다.

정여울, 『아주 보통의 연애』, 문학동네, 2011

Why do we need "some other thing"—as medium of communication, as protective camouflage, as roles we can reduce ourselves to—besides our own selves? In this era where direct experience is no longer essential, people confine themselves in mechanical roles and replace their physical beings with "digital avatars" with made-up identities. It is this struggle of "the original-self" to make themselves their own shadows or alter-egos that constitutes the running theme of Baek's short stories.

Jung Yeo-ul, *Very Ordinary Love Affair*,
Munhakdongne Publishing, 2011

K-픽션 024
연애의 감정학

2019년 2월 15일 초판 1쇄 발행

지은이 백영옥 | 옮긴이 제이미 챙, 신혜빈 | 펴낸이 김재범
기획위원 전성태, 정은경, 이경재
편집 김형욱, 강민영 | 관리 강초민, 홍희표 | 디자인 나루기획
인쇄·제책 굿에그커뮤니케이션 | 종이 한솔PNS
펴낸곳 (주)아시아 | 출판등록 2006년 1월 27일 제406-2006-000004호
주소 경기도 파주시 회동길 445(서울 사무소: 서울특별시 동작구 서달로 161-1 3층)
전화 02.821.5055 | 팩스 02.821.5057 | 홈페이지 www.bookasia.org
ISBN 979-11-5662-173-7(set) | 979-11-5662-401-1(04810)
값은 뒤표지에 있습니다.

K-Fiction 024
How to Break Up Like a Winner

Written by Baek Young-ok | **Translated by** Jamie Chang, Shin Hye-bin
Published by ASIA Publishers | 445, Hoedong-gil, Paju-si, Gyeonggi-do, Korea
(Seoul Office:161-1, Seodal-ro, Dongjak-gu, Seoul, Korea)
Homepage Address www.bookasia.org | **Tel**.(822).821.5055 | **Fax**.(822).821.5057
First published in Korea by ASIA Publishers 2019
ISBN 979-11-5662-173-7(set) | 979-11-5662-401-1(04810)

바이링궐 에디션 한국 대표 소설

한국문학의 가장 중요하고 첨예한 문제의식을 가진 작가들의 대표작을 주제별로 선정!
하버드 한국학 연구원 및 세계 각국의 한국문학 전문 번역진이 참여한 번역 시리즈!
미국 하버드대학교와 컬럼비아대학교 동아시아학과, 캐나다 브리티시컬럼비아대학교 아시아
학과 등 해외 대학에서 교재로 채택!

바이링궐 에디션 한국 대표 소설 set 3

K-포엣 시리즈는 계속됩니다.
리스트에 변동이 있을 수 있습니다.